"Let's tal[k]"

It was as if Cory's life flashed before his eyes. The past few months seemed like forever, and today was moving at light speed.

He gulped. This was it. The moment he'd been both dreaming about and dreading. "Us?"

Daphne looked down into her cup, which made him even more nervous. "I was thinking about it last night, and I hope this isn't being too forward, but I really like you."

Her face turned a bit pink, and he hoped it was because she was thinking about the same thing that flashed through his mind—the short kiss they'd shared before they were so rudely interrupted.

"I hope you feel the same way, so I want to ask you where you want to go with our relationship." She looked up at him. "We do have a relationship, don't we?"

An award-winning author of more than forty books, **Gail Sattler** lives in Vancouver, BC (where you don't have to shovel rain), with her husband, three sons, two dogs and a lizard who is quite cuddly for a reptile. Gail enjoys making music with a local jazz band and a community orchestra. When she's not writing or making music, Gail likes to sit back with a hot coffee and a good book.

Books by Gail Sattler

Love Inspired Heartsong Presents

The Best Man's Secret
The Best Man's Holiday Romance
Dating the Best Man

GAIL SATTLER

Dating the Best Man

HEARTSONG
PRESENTS

Recycling programs
for this product may
not exist in your area.

 LOVE INSPIRED BOOKS

ISBN-13: 978-0-373-48777-6

Dating the Best Man

Copyright © 2015 by Gail Sattler

www.Harlequin.com

Printed in U.S.A.

The grass withers, the flower fades,
but the word of our God stands forever.
—*Isaiah* 40:8

To my mom, Helen.
Because you saw the writing process on this one
up close and personal. Yes, that's really how it works.

Chapter 1

As Daphne Carruthers dabbed the tissue to her eyes she looked around at all the other women seated nearby, who were also wiping their eyes. Women watching the wedding ceremony with men who were obviously boyfriends or husbands. Not their brothers. She wasn't so lucky.

She turned to Rick, sitting beside her with his arms crossed and scowling at the latest of their friends to get married. Any moment she expected to hear him mumble, "Sucker."

Again she turned to the front as Brad and Kayla faced the pastor, their attendants at their sides.

If the wedding wasn't so romantic, the picture could have been funny. Kayla and her maid of honor and one bridesmaid stood at about five foot five inches, give or take an inch, which was several inches taller than Daphne. Brad and his groomsman were about five foot ten, but the best man, Cory, towered above them all. She didn't know his exact height, but she would have guessed that Cory was taller than her brother by three or four inches, and her brother was six feet even.

She wondered if he had ever played basketball.

She also wondered how often he'd been asked that very thing.

Because Cory was the quiet one in her brother's group of friends, she didn't know the answer. In fact, she didn't even know how Cory and Rick had met. All she knew about him was that he was a forest ranger, which was probably a good job for him because of his size. He didn't need to be afraid of the bears; the bears were probably afraid of him.

The pastor's happy voice rang out through the building. "I pronounce you husband and wife! You may now kiss the bride."

Before the pastor finished speaking, Brad had already lifted Kayla's veil. After the pastor's words he kept kissing her until the pastor cleared his throat, not once, but twice. A number of the ladies giggled and a couple of the men hooted. When they finally separated, the pastor introduced them as Mr. and Mrs. Kendall and they began their trip down the aisle as a married couple.

Daphne sniffled again. "Isn't that romantic?" she whispered to Rick.

Rick grunted, then actually muttered, "Sucker."

She wanted to poke him with her elbow, but it was pointless.

While Brad and Kayla and their attendants posed in front of the old brick building for a few pictures, Daphne stood back with Rick. The photographer moved the bridal party back to the door, where he could pose everyone on the steps. He positioned Cory to stand one stair lower than everyone else, so his head was only slightly higher than his friends in the wedding party. Friends and family snapped photos behind the photographer.

"Are you going to get any closer?" Rick asked when she snapped a few pictures from where they stood.

"No, I'm good."

As a young couple beside them exchanged a quick kiss, Rick stiffened. Daphne knew he was wary of love. Personally, he'd seen too many women fall in love with his policeman's uniform, then be unable to handle the life of the man beneath the uniform. Because her brother was single—and planned to stay that way—he was happy to be at her side when needed, and that was what Daphne wanted. No one messed with Rick; therefore, no one would ever mess with her.

Not ever again. At least they wouldn't if they knew Rick was never far away.

And that was why, as brother and sister, they were together as the only non-couple at Brad and Kayla's wedding.

From her purse, Daphne's phone sounded with the tone that she'd received a new text message.

"I can't believe you didn't turn that off," Rick grumbled, then automatically patted his pocket where he kept his own phone, which was always set to vibrate.

"I don't know who would text me now." The few people who would text her were either already there or knew she was at a wedding today.

She pulled her phone out of her purse. "This is odd. It's Frank, my boss." Her stomach tightened. She'd applied for a promotion into the marketing department. Word had it that the final decision was now between her and one other employee. "I don't know why he's sending me a message today. This is going to be either really good or really bad." She sucked in a deep breath and pressed the screen to read his message.

"Which is it?"

Daphne read in silence, then read it again to let the words sink in. "There's a chamber of commerce dinner tomorrow, and Frank suddenly can't go. He says he asked Ken, the other guy who wants the job in marketing, and Ken said he won't work weekends. Frank says the job is mine if I go."

"That's good, isn't it?"

"I…I think so."

For the first time all afternoon Rick smiled. "What's not good? Aren't those things usually at a five-star restaurant downtown? All you need to do is smile and listen to a few boring speeches."

She gulped. "That's true, but I can't go alone. Frank says I need a date, and you're working tomorrow."

Rick's smile dropped. "This means the difference between getting that job and not getting it, right?"

"It sounds like it. These things don't happen often, but when they do, they're important. I think the point is that he'll give the job to whoever makes it a priority, and Ken blew it. I need to go." She gulped again. "And not alone. He was specific about bringing a date. I don't know why."

"Does he know you're not dating?"

"Not really. Everyone knows I'm not in a relationship, but no one knows why. What do I do? I really need that promotion."

"Are you ready to go out on a date without me?"

She shook her head. "I don't know." Besides work, she'd only been out in public with one person—her brother—since the terrible day that had changed her life. Now, six months later, the thought of being alone with a man still made her feel like throwing up.

"Your words say yes, but your head says no. I'm inclined to go with your head."

Daphne pressed her hand over her heart, which was pounding. "You're right. I'm really scared. But I need this promotion. If I ever want to move out of Mom and Dad's house I need a better job, and this one is perfect." She also needed to show her parents that she was okay, even if she wasn't, to stop them from constantly worrying about her.

"Then you'll need to go with someone I know. Someone we both can trust."

It took everything within her to not shake her head. The few who knew understood, but being un-

derstood didn't help her right now. This was her worst
fear come to life: she was going to be alone in a
crowd of strangers, knowing only one person. But
if her brother knew the man who would accompany
her, then she didn't need to be afraid when the event
was all over.

Not like the last time.

She cleared her throat. "I really need to do this.
But all your cop friends are working tomorrow, too,
aren't they?"

Rick nodded. "Yeah. There's a big heavy metal
rock concert at the park, and everyone who didn't
have a regular shift is working overtime to make sure
there's no trouble."

Daphne's mind went blank, so she turned to watch
the wedding party.

While the photographer positioned the wedding
party again, Brad reached out and gently tucked a
stray lock of Kayla's hair out of her eyes. The dreamy
smile they exchanged was the thing fairy tales were
made of.

That was what Daphne had wanted once. But now
she didn't think she could ever let her guard down
to take the risk.

The photographer snapped a few more pictures,
sent the attendants away, then motioned for the bride's
and groom's parents to take their turn with the happy
couple.

The bridesmaid and matron of honor joined their
boyfriend and husband, respectively. The groomsman
joined his wife. Cory stood alone, looking quite lost.

Rick waved one hand in the air until Cory noticed him. Cory looked from side to side, probably checking in case Rick was motioning to someone else. Then, satisfied Rick meant him, Cory walked toward them.

"There's your man," Rick said to Daphne, then turned to Cory when he reached them. "Cory, my friend, are you busy tomorrow?"

Cory Bellanger opened his mouth to reply but no words came out.

As Rick asked the question, Daphne's face turned from a cute pink to ghostly white. The change was so sudden and so drastic he thought she was going to faint.

He reached toward her in case she toppled. "Are you okay? Do you need to sit down?" If she sank to the grass she'd probably get green stains on her pretty dress. He glanced at the church's park bench, but it was halfway across the property.

Instead of leaning toward him, Daphne stepped back, wobbling slightly but managing to keep upright.

Rick's face tightened. His fingers clenched into fists, then opened stiffly.

As Cory looked into his friend's face, the question drifted back to his mind. "No. I'm not busy tomorrow. Why? What's up?"

Rick turned to Daphne, so Cory did the same.

Daphne cleared her throat and turned her head, but as she spoke she didn't meet his eyes. "I need someone to join me at a last-minute business dinner tomorrow night. Can you come with me? Dress is business casual."

As Cory waited for more details, he fought to keep himself from grinning like a kid who'd just gotten everything he wanted for Christmas.

A year ago he'd wanted to ask Daphne out, but she'd been going steady with another guy. Then suddenly it was over, and just as suddenly it was almost as though she dropped off the face of the planet. Whenever he'd asked Rick about her all Rick said was that she'd had an accident and needed some time to herself. That had been months.

No one had ever told him what kind of injury. The first time he'd seen her since her breakup, she'd looked pretty much the same, although thinner. But looks aside, whatever had happened had made her very withdrawn. Her spirit had dimmed.

And the smallest mention of Daphne to her brother turned his friend into a mother bear protecting her cubs. Rick had made it clear that she wasn't interested in dating him and that had been the end of that.

Now, six months later, apparently that had changed. Except, even though she'd asked him, she looked like a scared rabbit with an eagle circling overhead.

She quickly told him where the dinner was and then clutched her purse to her chest. "Excuse me. I need to phone my boss back." She'd barely finished speaking before she dashed off. When she reached the bench he'd seen earlier, she sat, pulled her cell phone out of her purse and made a call.

Cory turned to Rick. "Is she okay?"

"Not really. You need to stay with her every minute, and not let her out of your sight. Like a bodyguard. Do I make myself clear?"

"Bodyguard? I don't understand." His stomach clenched. "Does this have something to do with her last boyfriend? Is she afraid of him coming after her?"

"Something like that."

Cory again waited for more details but none came.

Rick stiffened and assumed the stance, every inch a cop on alert. "And if I hear you did something to scare or hurt her, I'll forget I'm a cop and break your arm. Maybe both arms. Don't forget that."

The hairs on the back of Cory's neck stood on end. Whatever happened to Daphne had been more than a car accident injury, as everyone had assumed. It was personal. Very personal. Now, if he ever saw her old boyfriend, maybe he'd be the one breaking arms.

Cory shook his head to rid himself of the thought. That was exactly what he couldn't do, for so very many reasons. "She'll be safe with me. You don't have to worry."

"This is really important to her. That's the only reason she's going. Don't forget that, either."

He wasn't really sure what Rick was saying, but if he had to act a part as well as be her protector, he would do that.

They both watched as Daphne finished her call then tucked her phone into her purse.

Slowly, she stood and began to walk toward them. While she did, he couldn't help but really look at her because it had been so long since he'd seen her, and now he could just watch without being noticeable.

Her hair had grown longer and somehow seemed darker; not just dark brown, but almost black. It hung past her shoulders, straight instead of slightly wavy. Instead of bangs, it was now parted to the side.

From a distance her dark hair seemed the same shade as the frames of her dark glasses, contrasting with her pale skin, telling him that she hadn't been outside much, if at all, since the last time he'd seen her six months ago.

She'd also lost weight. She'd had a little bit of weight on her frame before, just right to give her some curves, but now she was too thin. He didn't think she'd done it on purpose. She'd never been shy about eating, not like other women he knew who were perpetually on a diet.

As she continued to move closer, he kept watching. The weight loss emphasized her high cheekbones and slightly long nose, something that had always embarrassed her. Not that he understood why anything on such a gorgeous face could embarrass her.

He wanted to feed her. For someone so short, probably more than a foot shorter than he was, being so thin made her look almost waiflike.

Since he was joining her for dinner tomorrow, maybe he could start a real friendship—and help get her back to what she'd been before whatever had happened.

As she joined them she broke into a big grin. "Everything is good." This time she looked up at him as she spoke, right into his eyes. When her smile deepened Cory felt his heart beat faster, which was ridiculous. "In fact, it's really good. I got the promotion. He's going to make the announcement to the rest of the staff on Monday."

He wanted to suggest that he take her out for a celebration, but something told him this wasn't the right time. Until he found out what had caused her to withdraw, common sense told him to tread lightly.

He looked down at her. She looked so small and fragile. Or maybe he felt that way because of the warnings he'd just received.

"Congratulations on the promotion. I'll do my best to fit in with the crowd, but I'm not really sure what to wear. What exactly is business casual? I don't have to return the tux to the rental place until Monday, but I'd guess it's too dressy. Besides…" He paused to tug at the bow tie. "It's not very comfortable. I don't own a suit. The closest I have is my dress uniform."

She smiled, this time at him, which gave him a really good feeling that maybe, just maybe, he stood a chance to spend more time with her than just the necessary business function. "While I'm sure you look very nice in your uniform, that's not necessary. Business casual just means nice slacks and a button-down shirt. Maybe a tie, but it's not necessary. Some of the men will wear ties, but not many since it's nearly summer. Just wear nice spring attire."

He smiled back. "My dress uniform has a tie, and the summer uniform has matching shorts. That should impress everyone. I've been told I have nice legs for a guy." Although he didn't have boots that weren't worn and stained. The dress uniform looked slightly ridiculous with shorts, and even more ridiculous if he had to wear shoes instead of hiking boots and wool socks.

Her cheeks turned the most charming shade of pink. "Ordinary pants are fine. I think they're calling you back for more pictures." She checked her watch. "It's also nearly time to go inside. The caterers are probably almost ready to serve the dinner. If you're busy and I don't see you later, I'll see you tomorrow. We need to be there about three o'clock to listen to a few boring speeches. I can pick you up. Is that okay?"

He tried not to grin like an idiot. Anything was okay as long as he could spend some time with her. "That's fine. See you then."

Chapter 2

Daphne pulled up in front of the address Rick had given her and drove into one of the assigned visitor spots. Rick lived in a high-rise building, probably more than twenty floors.

She'd deleted most of the contacts in her cell phone after dropping off of everyone's radar because she didn't want to answer all their questions. And she'd had good reason: for those she did answer, they didn't believe her. Now, for the first time in six months she'd actually added someone to her address book. Tomorrow she'd add back the people she'd seen again at the wedding who wanted to get back in touch. Texting was a good start, without getting too personal.

She swiped Cory's name. Rather than actually speak to him, she hit the prompt to text him.

I M here in front.

He answered within seconds.

B rite out.

Rick had told her that Cory lived on the seventh floor so she expected to wait for him to use the elevator, which would give her time to compose herself before she had to face him. She'd barely dropped her phone back into her purse when Cory walked out the main door.

Somehow he looked even better in regular clothes than the tuxedo he'd worn yesterday. Yesterday it had been obvious he hadn't been comfortable in the penguin suit, as Rick had called it. Today, Cory was definitely comfortable, walking with a long, easy stride that said he owned the space around him.

Yesterday, after Rick dropping the bomb that Cory was going to be her escort for the chamber of commerce dinner she'd been somewhat in a state of shock, so she hadn't been able to really look at him.

Most really tall men tended to be thin, but not Cory. His husky, fit frame filled out his clothes well. As he raised his arms to straighten his sunglasses, the flex caused a bulge of definition as the muscles of his upper arms filled out the confines of his shirt-sleeves, for a few moments making the sleeves tight. The man had muscles on his muscles.

Likewise, as he walked, the muscles in his thighs were clearly defined through the cloth of his pants.

Six months ago she would have teased him and asked him to go back to change into his shorts just so she could judge for herself if indeed he did have nice legs for a man, as he'd claimed.

She suspected he had been telling the truth.

Not only was he big, he was also good-looking—the epitome of the clichéd fairy tale of tall, dark, and handsome, except he was probably taller than Prince Charming ever dreamed. His dark complexion could have given him an exotic appearance, but he was too thick to be exotic. Big, square-jawed, with dark brown eyes that matched his dark brown hair, he could have been a modern-day Paul Bunyan without the beard.

She wished she could have been able to appreciate him from a distance, where she felt more comfortable. But that wasn't going to happen, at least not today. With that confident stride, it only took a minute for him to arrive beside her car.

He nodded to her through the window, then walked to the passenger door and opened it. Instead of sitting he looked in front of the seat and then looked at the back, then down to where his feet would be. He squatted and reached inside under the seat, engaged the lever and slid the seat back as far as it would go.

Frowning, he maneuvered himself into the chair and fastened the seat belt, then closed the car door. With his knees bent sharply, resting against the bottom of the glove box, and his head nearly touching the roof, he didn't look comfortable. He filled the seat completely, and then some.

He turned and smiled graciously. "Not bad for a small car. I'd bet you get really great gas mileage, don't you?"

Daphne stiffened. She hadn't had a passenger for a long time, and never one so tall or so broad. She hadn't considered the possibility that he wouldn't fit. All she'd thought about was that she wouldn't be able to be a passenger in a man's car, even if the man had been recommended by her brother. She needed the reassurance of having her own car—her means of escape if necessary.

Cory checked his watch, forcing her to notice the breadth of his wrists and the size of his hands—something else she hadn't noticed before.

She felt herself breaking into a cold sweat. More than ever, she questioned if she was doing the right thing.

"It's nearly two-thirty. I guess we should be going." He turned back to her. "You look nice. I wasn't sure if this is the kind of event where a man would buy a corsage for a lady, but since it's a business thing, I didn't. Maybe next time."

Unless it was her imagination, she thought Cory stiffened a bit and held his breath for a few seconds, until she replied.

"No. No corsage." She wasn't sure what he meant about a next time. As far as she knew, her boss would be able to attend the next chamber dinner, and she wouldn't need Cory to go with her. But just in case, she said nothing. Regardless of how she felt, he was doing her a favor by giving up his time and she needed to appreciate it.

While she drove to the restaurant Cory limited conversation to small talk, something she also appreciated. Not just because that meant he wasn't going to pry, but the unimportant chatter helped prepare her to interact in a crowd of strangers—something she hadn't done for a long time.

Since they arrived at the banquet hall fairly early, the lot had many empty spaces. He didn't comment when she circled three times to find the spot closest to the door.

Daphne remained seated while Cory extricated himself awkwardly from the car, mentally kicking herself for not finding a parking spot that would have allowed him to open the door all the way to give him more space. She told herself it would never happen again. Not because she would be more careful to park in the last spot of a row, but because she would never be going out with him again.

When he made it out, Daphne hustled around the car to stand beside him so they could walk to the door side by side. After all, they were together. Because they would be standing for a long time before they were seated for the dinner and speeches, she'd worn her most comfortable shoes, which were almost flat.

Standing across from Cory she'd obviously known he was very tall, but now, walking beside him, she felt like an elf. Even if she'd worn her tallest shoes and made her feet suffer through the affair, that wouldn't have made any difference. She would still have been a foot shorter than him. Even if he were barefoot, it wouldn't have helped.

The way he took steps that were unnaturally short for his size made her feel even worse that she couldn't match his pace. If he'd been walking with his normal long stride, she would have to jog to keep even with him.

"Don't worry," he said as he looked down at her. "I'm used to walking with people shorter than me."

"Do you know anyone taller than you? How tall are you, anyway?"

"Six four." He sighed. "I've met people taller. Just not many. Like, two."

Her guess had been off by an inch. It was hard to judge when looking up so high. She waited, anticipating him asking if she knew anyone shorter than herself. She had the same answer. She was the shortest in her circle of friends. Or the people she used to call friends.

As they walked in and waited for their turn to sign the register as invited guests, she felt the stares of people around them. She hoped they were just looking at Cory because he was so tall and good-looking, and not because they looked ridiculous together.

When she signed them in he looked at the growing crowd around them, then down at her. "I'd ask if you'd like to go sit down, but I have a feeling the reason we're here is so you can do some schmoozing."

"I suppose that's one way to describe it. Yes. I need to schmooze. Is that really a word?"

He shrugged his shoulders. "I have no idea. I see people holding drinks. Are you thirsty?"

"Yes, but I only want an iced tea, no alcohol. You can have both tickets." She held the drink tickets toward him, but before she'd raised them high enough for him to take them, he raised one palm to stop her.

"No, thank you. I'm going to have a soft drink. I'll be right back."

After he left her side, Daphne scanned the room. She saw a few people she knew and immediately felt more comfortable. While she continued to search the crowd for more familiar faces her attention kept being drawn back to Cory, standing in the short line at the bar. While he spoke with those around him he often glanced back at her, smiling whenever they made eye contact.

She didn't know if he was watching for her on his own, or if her ever-protective brother had told him to keep an eye on her. She wasn't sure if she'd be annoyed or comforted if that were the case.

One day she would have to get over it, but that day wasn't today.

"Daphne?" A female voice sounded from behind her. "Is that you? I haven't seen you for a dog's age. How are you?"

She spun to face a woman who worked for one of the other merchants in the strip mall where she worked.

She struggled to remember the woman's name. She couldn't. All she knew was that the woman worked at the book store at the other end of the strip.

The woman smiled. "It's Susan. I can see you didn't remember my name. That's okay. I know you don't go to many of these things."

Daphne smiled. "Actually this is my first time here. Usually, I've seen you at the mall merchants' meetings. I've been to a few of those with Frank."

Susan nodded. "I remember the last one, yes. When I saw your name today, I switched the name tags at the table so you'll be sitting with us. So tell me, how are things doing at the pet supply store?"

She didn't know if this was the time to announce her promotion from customer service to the marketing department, but then, it wouldn't matter to Susan, so she didn't. "Things are going well. How about you?"

"Great!" The sudden chorus in Susan's tone made Daphne flinch, and she hoped Susan hadn't noticed. Apparently she didn't, because Susan held out her left hand to flash a brilliant diamond ring at Daphne. "Xavier and I are getting married! We're going to have a big party at the store, and everyone from all the stores in the mall is invited to drop in to celebrate with us."

Automatically, Daphne looked around for Xavier, who owned the book store where Susan worked. Last she'd seen, he'd been talking to Cory in the bar lineup, and now they were coming back together.

Cory handed her the iced tea she'd requested and Xavier handed Susan a glass of wine.

"Congratulations," Daphne said as all four clicked their glasses in a toast.

"And who is this?" Susan beamed as she looked up at Cory, gaining a stern look of reproach from Xavier when she nearly started to drool.

"This is Cory," Daphne said.

At the intro, Cory smiled and nodded at both of them.

"And he is your…?"

The question mentally smacked Daphne. She'd seen it before—newly engaged women wanting to spread the joy of romance to everyone they met. Sadly, not every supposedly happy relationship ended with a happily-ever-after ending.

She looked up at Cory, obligated to fill in the blank. She really didn't know what to say. Officially he was her escort assigned by her brother. Not a date. She didn't even know him all that well. She'd only spent time with him as part of a group with her brother's friends. She'd talked to him one-on-one a few times, but it hadn't been often, mostly only within the group. To say something that didn't lessen the generosity of him giving up his day for her, she had to say something.

"Friend. Cory is my friend."

Sparing her from being prompted to say more, the manager from the sporting goods store joined Cory and Xavier, starting another one of his famous fish stories. The second he had their attention Susan nudged her. "What happened to that blond fellow you were going out with? I thought you'd be here with him. Word had it that you were on the verge of getting engaged, too."

At the mention of Alex, Daphne's world started collapsing around her. Her vision narrowed, her breath became tight, and she felt herself starting to shake.

Before she fell and embarrassed herself, she reached for Cory. Once she had the best grip she could on his wide arm, she tried her best to smile politely at Susan while she cleared her throat, trying to pull herself together. "We split up."

As her fingers began to go numb, her glass disappeared out of her hand and Cory's deep voice whispered in her ear. "I'm going to put my arm around your waist and take you away, where you can sit. Would you like that?"

All she could do was nod.

"Excuse us," he said to everyone around him. "I think Daphne and I need to talk."

"Oh, dear," Susan muttered. "I hope I haven't gotten you in trouble with your new boyfriend."

"Don't worry," Cory replied. "Everything is fine. We just need a little time alone. Excuse us."

Cory led her to a table in the corner, where he helped her sit. "Do you need to put your head down? Do you need to go home?"

"No. I'll be okay. I just need a couple of minutes." Alex wasn't here, and he wasn't coming here. She repeated that to herself a number of times, and told herself she was going to be fine. She could carry on. She needed to get on with her life, and this was the day she was going to make that happen.

Slowly the world returned to normal, except for her

feeling of profound embarrassment. "I'm fine now. I'm so sorry."

"Don't be sorry. I've seen panic attacks before. Do you want to talk about it?"

She didn't really, but she'd put him in a spot, and she'd been told talking about it would help. She'd just convinced herself that today was the day she was going to start moving forward. Now was the time to put her money where her mouth was.

She cleared her throat. "Are you sure you want to hear this?"

He reached forward as if to grip her hands, looked down at them and then folded his hands in front of himself on the table.

"If you want to talk, then I'd like to listen. Go ahead."

Cory waited in silence while Daphne struggled with her thoughts. From the way she went into a panic attack when her ex's name was mentioned, he had a bad feeling the story was going to be about a very bad breakup. But the longer she took to think about it, the picture in his mind grew worse and worse.

Rick's words, and his instructions not to let Daphne out of his sight, played in his mind. Now Cory could see why. She was terrified. The moment the other woman had innocently mentioned her ex's name, he'd thought Daphne might crumple to the floor.

When she finally spoke, her voice came out in barely a whisper. "Before you think the worst, he didn't actually rape me. But it was close. Very close."

Rape. Just the word tightened his gut. It was worse than he'd thought it would be. He couldn't think of anything to say, so he remained silent.

"We'd been out for a late dinner and, as Susan said, he proposed to me at the restaurant. It was classically romantic. He even gave me a ring. By the time we were done we were the last people out. He'd parked in the back corner of the lot saying at the time he didn't want to risk anyone banging the paint on his doors."

Right away, Cory got the mental picture of why, and it had nothing to do with paint. Sometimes when a guy did a romantic thing for a woman in public, often he had plans for what she would now do with him in private.

He gritted his teeth, forcing himself to remain silent.

"Instead of driving away, he wanted to do other things. He made it very clear that since we were officially engaged, I owed it to him to do everything he wanted. When I refused, he forced himself on me. It was awful. I thought I loved him, but he was hurting me."

Cory couldn't stay silent any longer. "You don't have to say more. I can't imagine how hard this is for you to talk about. Especially here."

She shook her head. "No, I need to get this out. I've been told I need to talk about it, but I haven't been able to. It's actually easier here. I think it's because I know I'm safe in the crowd, yet there's no one close enough to hear what I say. If you want to listen." She cleared her throat and wiped her eyes with her sleeve.

Cory's stomach did a nosedive into his shoes. He didn't really want to listen, but something inside made him. Like arriving at a train wreck, when people couldn't do anything but still stayed to watch the carnage. "Go on."

"Since we were so late, Rick, being Rick, was worried, so he phoned me. Of course I didn't answer my phone, I was trying to defend myself and not succeeding. Rick was worried we'd had an accident, so he tracked the GPS signal on my phone. When he got there the windows were all fogged. He couldn't see in and I couldn't see out. I was trying so hard to get away, but I couldn't. Alex had me totally overpowered, and he was totally out of control. He was hurting me, and I was screaming, but he wouldn't stop. At the last second before…you know, the side window shattered. It was Rick."

The picture in his mind made Cory grip the side of the table so hard he thought it might crumble. Words failed him.

"He hauled Alex out and started punching him until I scrambled out of the car. Rick took one look at me and threw Alex to the ground and left him there. Rick wrapped his jacket around me to cover me up and then he tried to stop the bleeding. Alex scrambled back in his car and took off, and Rick took me to the hospital. The next day, Rick was on duty so he went to Alex's place in uniform, but Alex was gone. Rick knew where he worked, so he went there, but he'd called in sick that morning. And soon after that, Alex was completely gone."

"You mean he just disappeared? He's got to be somewhere."

"Rick asked Alex's friends but no one would tell him anything. My best friend was his sister. She didn't know, either—and I couldn't tell her what had happened. She blamed me. I know she did."

Daphne paused, looked down, took a deep breath, then looked back up at him. "His boss just said he'd moved on, and wouldn't give details. A week later a florist delivered some flowers with a note saying 'I'm sorry' but they wouldn't tell me where the order came from.

"The police, except for Rick, don't consider him dangerous. Rick wants me to press charges, but with Alex gone, I decided to wait. For now, I need to get on with my life, not to keep going over what I can't change. I'm trying to put it behind me." She clasped and unclasped her hands.

"The policemen said hopefully he would show up, since they don't have the manpower to actively search for him without a warrant. When he surfaces, I can decide then what to do. It's been six months, so I guess he's moved on with his life. Maybe he's even left the country. I don't know. Now I don't even know if I want him to be found and get everything dragged through the courts. Yet at the same time, I want him to be punished."

He'd heard that rape and rape-related court cases were tough. Everything had to be brought into the open, with all the wounds opened and exposed and analyzed. He didn't know anyone who'd been through it, only what he'd read in the papers. Much of the painful details would become public knowledge, although he was sure some would be kept private. He couldn't imagine what it would be like to be so violated. "Are you okay now?" he asked out loud, although he expected she was really far from okay.

"I've been working on it." She gave a lame, self-depreciating laugh. "But as you can see, some days are better than others. Today turned out to be one of the not better days. I'd decided with the promotion it was time to get on with my life. It doesn't look like I'm doing all that well. I'm so sorry."

Cory shook his head. "Don't be sorry. Ever. You've been through a lot." He could see that she'd have trust issues with men for a long time, and now he understood why she'd insisted on taking her own car and finding a spot close to the door. He also understood why Rick was reluctant to leave her side, and why Rick had chosen him to be with her today, even with a warning.

Now that he knew, he feared that if he ever came face to face with Alex it would spell disaster, both for Alex and for himself.

Daphne looked toward the growing crowd. "I think it's time to rejoin the party." She checked her watch. "We haven't done much schmoozing, and it's nearly time for the meal and the speeches."

"I think the most important thing is that you showed up. If you're really okay, let's go to our assigned seats. If not, I'm okay if you want to leave."

She shook her head. "No. I need to do this. I'm

safe here. There's nothing here to hurt me, and I have every reason to stay. Like I said, I need to get on with my life. I can't let Alex control me anymore. Let's go join everybody."

They stood at the same time. "You might want to go to the ladies' bathroom and fix your makeup. I'll meet you back at our table."

"Of course. Thanks."

She dashed off before he could say she had nothing to thank him for.

As he sat at the table there were two people he hadn't met, but Xavier and his fiancée, whose name he couldn't remember, were at the same table.

The woman leaned forward over the table to him. "Is Daphne okay?"

She really wasn't, but it wasn't any of this woman's business. "No worries. Everything is fine." Or, as fine as it could be, which wasn't fine at all. "Excuse me. I need to go get a couple of drinks for Daphne and me."

While he waited in line he thought about what he could do to help, but he didn't know what.

Daphne arrived at the table at the same time as he did. She slid into the chair beside his as if nothing had happened.

She turned to give him the most beautiful smile he'd ever seen. "Did I miss anything?"

"I don't think so. It looks like they're going to start some of the speeches."

Her chair was angled to have her back toward the stage and podium. Before he realized what she was doing, she stood, pushed her chair until it was beside his and sat again.

They were so close that to the unknowing eye, they would have seemed like a couple. As he wished they could be, now even more than before.

She turned to him, smiling, yet her eyes seemed sad. "Are you ready for this?"

"Yes," he said, but his brain screamed *no*. Something in his life had changed. Something he didn't think he was ready for at all.

Maybe, just maybe, he might be falling a little in love.

Chapter 3

Just as she did every day as she left the office, Daphne slipped into her car and immediately locked the door. But today, before she started the engine, she looked up to the second floor, to the window of what was now her private office.

This was it. The start of her new life. With her first pay stub at her new salary tucked into her purse, she now knew how much she would be earning after taxes. After a few months she could either move out on her own, or she could continue to live with her parents until she squirreled away enough money for a down payment on a small condo.

Six months ago she would have called a few friends and gone out to celebrate. Or, she would have gone out with Alex to make plans for their future. Or maybe both.

Now neither was a consideration. Out of fear,

she'd turned herself into a hermit. Her only outlet for months had been a post-trauma therapy group. It had helped a lot, but at the same time, listening to the other women's stories had added a new level of fear.

The one time she'd gone out to a business event without her brother she'd almost had a meltdown, then a man she'd barely known had helped her pull herself together. *Cory.* She didn't know what a forest ranger did exactly, but probably calming small and frightened animals was part of Cory's job. He'd taken over without being pushy or threatening, providing a safe escape while taking her aside to help her get her bearings. He had a gentle way about him. Like a Great Dane, he knew his power, so he had nothing he needed to prove.

As Daphne continued to stare up at the window, her phone sang out.

She had no idea who it could be. This time it couldn't be her boss because she'd bade him goodbye for the weekend only minutes ago. Her friends had stopped calling months ago.

The display on her phone showed the caller to be Cory.

Her first thought was to let it go to voice mail, but she couldn't do that. Not after he'd been key to her keeping her promotion—and her dignity. She owed him. Big time.

Her finger shook as she swiped the keypad to answer.

"Hi, Cory. I was just thinking of you."

Silence hung for a few seconds. "Really? Good things, I hope."

She doubted that comparing him to a large and somewhat loose-jowled slobbery dog would be taken as a compliment, so she just said, "Yes."

Another silence hung, then he cleared his throat. "I was just talking to Rick and he said you'd be getting off work about now. I was wondering if you'd like to join me for dinner. Nothing fancy. In fact, I was kind of thinking of going to that restaurant on the second floor of the mall and getting a table on the balcony overlooking all the action."

She knew the place. It was busy and always crowded, but yet the spot he mentioned was nice, if a person didn't mind that all the shoppers could see you as they walked by, or all the background noise. It would be a protected spot in the middle of mayhem.

Since Cory had already spoken to Rick, Rick knew where they were going, and a reasonable time that she'd be home. He'd time it to the minute.

But this time, unlike the last time she'd met a man for a dinner engagement, she would have her own car. She wouldn't need to get into any enclosed spaces with anyone where there were no means of escape.

Daphne sucked in a deep breath and reminded herself that getting the promotion was the start of reclaiming her life. She needed to break out of the fish bowl in which she'd enclosed herself. She'd prayed for God to help her, and maybe this was how it was going to happen. One small step, but still a step. All she had to do was to accept the help He gave her.

"Yes, that sounds nice." Terrifying, but nice. She checked her watch. "I could be there in fifteen minutes. Would that work for you?"

"Yes. Fifteen minutes would be perfect. I'll see you there."

It was done. Tonight would be her night of celebration. At the mall she would be safe in the crowd. Especially if she had a watchdog with her. And with her own car, she didn't need to fear the watchdog. She only had to feed him.

Inwardly, Daphne cringed at her thoughts. She needed to stop thinking of Cory like a large dog. But then again, not a dog, he was more like a bear.

She tried to stop the mental picture. She had no reason not to trust him, since Rick trusted him. She couldn't understand why Cory had asked her to join him for dinner. Unless, as repayment for being her escort to the chamber dinner, he wanted her help selecting a gift for his mother for Mother's Day. Therefore, a restaurant at the mall made sense.

That, she could handle. She also would pick something up for her mother tonight, instead of buying it online and having it shipped as she'd planned.

Before she started the car, she sent a quick text to Rick telling him she'd agreed to meet Cory at the mall for dinner and a little shopping.

She made her way there in good time and even found a good parking spot close to the main door.

Venturing through the mall wasn't as bad as she'd feared. Rather than feel terrified by all the strangers, instead she felt safe buried in the crowd. Confidence buoyed, she rode up the escalator to the second level and entered the restaurant Cory had chosen. He was easy to find. Even sitting, his head towered above everyone else already seated, making her realize he never slouched, standing or sitting.

She would never have to worry about losing him.

Not that she planned to spend any more time with him once she helped him with his shopping.

He smiled and waved as soon as he saw her. Her stomach made a crazy flutter and she couldn't tell if it was fear or something else.

Fortunately he didn't stand as she weaved through the people waiting for a table.

She quickly slipped into the chair across from him. "Have you been waiting long?" She leaned to tuck her purse between her feet. "They're starting a waiting list."

He shook his head. "I've only been here a few minutes."

Looking at the half-empty coffee cup in front of him, apparently he either drank his coffee very fast or the restaurant served it lukewarm. "Today will be a good day for shopping for Mother's Day. I saw lots of sale signs."

He turned to look past the crowd, past the balcony that overlooked the mall. "That's good."

"Do you have something specific that you're thinking of, or are you going to browse for ideas? My mom likes to knit, so this year I want to buy her a pattern and some yarn to make a sweater for Missy. It will keep her busy over the summer."

Cory raised his cup and swirled his coffee. "I've already bought my mom a gift card from the gas station, all I have to do is buy a stamp and put it in the mailbox." He raised the cup to his lips and began to sip the lukewarm brew.

"You give your mother gas?"

His eyes widened and he choked. He pressed his fist to his mouth as he coughed and then clunked the cup down onto the table so fast some coffee splashed out.

As soon as she realized what she'd said, Daphne covered her mouth with her hands. "I'm so sorry. I didn't mean that the way it came out."

He laughed then began to cough again. "Actually she's said worse about me. Don't worry about it."

Watching him recover, she wondered if he was serious or kidding about what worse things his mother would say, which then made her wonder what kind of relationship he had with his mother. Her own mother had cautioned her to look at the way a man treated his mother before she got into a serious relationship, because the way a man treated his mother would be similar to the way he treated his wife—with love and respect or not.

From what she'd seen Alex had a good relationship with his mother, but now that she thought about it, his mother had made jokes about always giving Alex whatever he wanted, and being so glad Daphne was doing the same. Maybe that was why the first time Daphne had said no to him, it had thrown him over the edge.

Cory turned to focus his attention on calling a waitress for more napkins, so Daphne focused her attention on him. At his size and obvious strength, she couldn't imagine what Cory could do if his temper flared or if he didn't get what he thought he deserved.

She cleared her throat. "Tell me about your mother. Why would you give your mother a gas card for Mother's Day?"

"Because my mother isn't very good with money," he muttered as he caught the waitress's attention. "She needs practical things."

At his words a million thoughts ran through her mind, the foremost was his relationship with his mother in general.

But really, it didn't matter. She'd planned to pay back his kindness by helping him select a gift and then they would go their separate ways.

Except, he wasn't buying a gift. He'd selected what he was going to give his mother already. She would have to repay him some other way.

She already knew he lived in an apartment. She didn't know if he was alone or with a friend, but she did know he was single.

Maybe she could bake him some cookies.

She cleared her throat. "Do you like chocolate?"

He broke out into a big grin. "I do. Why?"

Before she could answer, the server appeared with a handful of new napkins. "Are you folks ready to order?" The young woman stood above her, pencil poised above the order pad.

Daphne hadn't even picked up the menu. But she

didn't want to spend the whole evening with Cory at the restaurant. "I'll have what he's having."

Cory's eyebrows quirked. "But you don't know what I'm having. We never talked about it."

"I trust you." At her words her heart skipped a beat. She trusted him to choose a meal. After that she would work on trusting him for other things, too. She needed to do that. After all, if her brother trusted him, then she could trust him, too.

Cory cleared his throat. "I'll have the double burger with mushrooms. Super-size the fries with a side of gravy. This comes with coleslaw, too, doesn't it?"

"Yes, it does." The server turned to Daphne. "Are you sure you want what he's having?"

She felt her cheeks turn warm. "I'll take the same burger platter, but the regular portions. I only want a single burger and no gravy on my fries."

The server bit her lower lip, very unsuccessful at hiding her grin. "Would you also like coffee, the same as him? That only comes in one size."

Daphne nodded. "Sure."

When the server left, Cory turned to Daphne. "I didn't mean to embarrass you. I eat a lot, especially on Friday at the end of the week. I don't know why that is, I'm just more hungry on Fridays."

All she could do was look at him. Even though he wasn't fat, he was probably double her weight. It would only be natural that he would eat twice as much as she did, even on a normal day when he wasn't hungry. With the small portions they'd been served last weekend at the chamber of commerce dinner, he must have picked up something to eat on the way home.

She wondered if Cory's mother seemed to have difficulty with money because she still hadn't recovered from the cost of feeding him in his teenaged years.

"It's okay. I don't know why I wasn't expecting that, but I should have. I can't imagine feeding you as a child. Do you have brothers and sisters as big as you?"

A look of regret showed in his expression before he turned away so she couldn't see his face. "No. I was an only child."

She waited to hear more, but a silence hung between them until he leaned back in his chair and crossed his arms over his chest. "Why did you ask earlier if I like chocolate?"

It had made sense at the time, but now she felt silly. "Since I'm obviously not helping you with buying any gifts today, I thought maybe I might make you some chocolate-chip cookies to say thank you for sacrificing your weekend and going with me to the chamber of commerce dinner."

"As much as I like home-made cookies, you don't have to do that. It was good going out with you." He paused. "In fact, I'd like to go out with you again."

The world turned to ice and her vision began to narrow into a tunnel. So she wouldn't have a repeat of what happened at the chamber banquet, she forced herself to take in a long, deep breath and then another until the dizziness abated. Fortunately she was sitting, so she didn't have to worry as much about making a fool of herself again until that happened.

Earlier today she'd promised herself, and God, that she was going to get on with her life. Apparently, God was calling her to step up to the plate.

Daphne cleared her throat and hoped her words sounded more sincere than she felt. "Sure. I'd like that."

Cory smiled, oblivious to how she was feeling. "Great. How about tomorrow? I can pick you up for lunch and we can go do something in the afternoon."

She tried not to let her head swim. She told herself that Cory wasn't Alex. It was time to do what her therapist said, and to stop letting the fear control her.

"Sure. That sounds…" She couldn't say fun. "Good. That sounds good."

At that moment the server appeared with their meals.

Hunger had deserted her. She wondered if Cory might want to eat most of her meal, since he was already digging into his own with fervor.

But then, watching him eat with such enjoyment did make her wonder what she was missing. As well, she wasn't going to do herself any favors by letting herself get weak with hunger.

Slowly she dipped a fry into the ketchup and nibbled it.

"Aren't they great?" Cory said between bites. "They use some kind of seasoning I've never tasted in any other place."

"Yes, they are good." As she ate more, her appetite returned and before she knew it she'd eaten her entire meal.

They'd barely had time to start a conversation when the server appeared with the bill.

Cory immediately gave the server a credit card. "We should go. There's a line. Are you ready to do that shopping?"

This time her world remained stable. She actually felt herself starting to smile. "Yes. I am. Thank you for dinner. First we can buy a stamp so you can mail that card to your mother, then we can shop till we drop."

Cory truly hated to shop. He really didn't understand the alleged joy of spending time in a store without having something specific to buy. When he went to the mall he followed his plan, and the only browsing he did was go to different stores for the same product to check the pricing.

Except for Christmas shopping when he got stuck in line, the longest he'd ever been inside a mall was twenty minutes.

Today they'd already been in the mall for half an hour, and he didn't feel like screaming and running for the door. He wouldn't call it fun, but he didn't mind Daphne's explorations of her shopping list. In fact, it was quite amusing. If he could control himself and not start laughing, the afternoon would be successful.

"What do you think of this one? Does it look too sissy?" She held up another tiny T-shirt. But it wasn't for a child.

The Missy that Daphne had mentioned earlier wasn't a little girl. Missy was a little dog.

"You really are asking the wrong person. I think they all look ridiculous. Dogs have fur coats. They don't need clothing."

"That's not the point," she grumbled, folding the pink dog shirt, complete with lace collar and sparkly stones glued onto it, and tucked it into her shopping basket.

Cory shook his head. He really didn't see any point to dressing dogs in people clothing. "I fail to see how a shirt for a dog is an appropriate Mother's Day gift."

"It's not. The pattern and the yarn are the present, because that's something fun for my mother to do. The shirt is just because it's cute."

When she'd mentioned buying yarn and a pattern, he hadn't thought anything of it. When he found out Missy was a dog he thought she was kidding, that it was some kind of knitting joke he didn't get. Obviously it was no joke; she really had picked out yarn and a pattern to knit a sweater for a dog. Since he'd already voiced his opinion on the T-shirt, Cory thought it best not to share his thoughts on knitting a sweater for an animal. Especially in the summer.

"Is that it for your list? If so, I need to go to the hardware store for some duct tape."

She looked up at him and grinned. She actually grinned. He felt his heart start to beat faster. "Duct tape? The handyman's secret weapon? All a man needs to fix anything is duct tape and WD-40. If it shouldn't move, and it does, use duct tape. If it needs to move and it doesn't, spray it."

Cory shook his head. "That's not true." He let his voice trail off. She'd been joking. "I just need duct tape." Although, at the moment he couldn't remember what exactly he needed it for, only that he did.

She was still smiling. This smiling Daphne was the woman who had captured his heart when she'd seen him out at a party with Rick, her brother, a year ago.

She was everything he'd dreamed of in the perfect woman. Well, not really perfect, but perfect for him. Kind. Generous. A sense of humor. Always willing to help others… As a fellow believer, she had a gentle way about her that had won him over the first time he'd met her. She was a little timid, but she looked small and delicate. And any reasons for her timidity were explained ten-fold by what happened with her ex-boyfriend.

Cory wanted to help protect her, but he didn't know what to do. He had no idea what it would feel like to have someone overpower him. One person tried that, once, unsuccessfully, and it had been a life-changing event for both of them—one he could never allow to happen again.

Mentally, Cory shook his head. He refused to let his past mistakes haunt him when his future now had the potential to be promising—both personally and professionally.

"Cory? Are you okay? Is something wrong?"

Daphne's words brought Cory's mind back to where it should have been. He shook his head to clear it and then turned to her. "Sorry. I was thinking about something else for a minute." He almost asked they could to go the hardware store now, but stopped before the words came out. Once they were done shopping she would want to go home, and that would be the end of their time together. "I can get the duct tape later. Was there something else you wanted to look at?"

Her cheeks turned the most adorable shade of pink. "I need to buy some new jeans. I've lost weight and everything I own is too loose."

"No," he said, speaking before he thought fully of what he was saying. "You don't need new clothes. You've gotten too skinny. You need to put the weight back on." If in a month they went to the beach, he would probably be able to count her ribs when she wore her bathing suit.

For a second her mouth dropped open. But instead of speaking, the light went out of her eyes and her head lowered so he couldn't see her face.

He wanted to kick himself. Not only were his words not uplifting or encouraging, they could have been taken as critical. It probably wasn't even politically correct to tell a woman she was too skinny, even if she was. But that wasn't the point. He needed to lift her up, not say something that could be taken as critical.

"I'm sorry. That didn't come out the way I meant. I meant that you've been under a lot of stress and it's taken a toll on you. Even before this happened you could have had five or ten pounds more on you, but now you're even—" he caught himself just in time before he said worse "—thinner. When you didn't have anything to spare to begin with."

She didn't raise her head, so he reached out to rest his hands on her shoulders. Her bony shoulders. "I—"

Before he could finish his sentence she gasped, jerked away from his touch and stared up at him with big, wide eyes, like a deer just before he hit it with his truck on the highway in the middle of the night.

Too late, he realized what he'd done. He'd scared her.

Quickly he hid his hands behind his back. "I'm sorry. I didn't think. I would never hurt you or force you to do something against your will."

Daphne sucked in a deep breath then stared at him. "I know that. I'm the one who should be sorry. I don't know why I did that. I've been going to counseling. I thought I was supposed to be over this by now. I didn't mean to spoil the evening. I think I should go home."

"No, don't go. How about if we just go sit on one of the benches in the mall and talk? And relax." Cory forced himself to breathe while she considered his request.

Finally the stiffness left her. "You're right. I have to stop running and face these moments and prove that nothing is going to happen. Let's pay for this stuff and we can go sit down."

They didn't talk much as they made their way to the cashier and then found a bench. But as they walked side by side, being in the crowd made him aware of just how tiny she was in comparison to the average person.

When they were finally sitting, he turned to Daphne, being very careful not to touch her, not even to let his leg brush her knee. "I have an idea. I can't blame you for being cautious, so how about if we do something about that. When I do information sessions at the campgrounds in the summer I warn people about the wild animals, and what to do if they come face to face with one. I usually start off with a joke about what if I and someone else came face to face with a bear. The joke is that I don't have to outrun the bear, I only have to outrun the other person. Get it?"

He waited for her to process his joke. When her eyes widened, he knew she got it. "I understand what you're saying about a bear, but this isn't the same situation."

"Not really, but the concept is that you don't have to overcome an attacker. You only have to know how to escape."

"I suppose that makes sense. But that's easier said than done."

Cory nodded. "I know. So let's start with the most basic. Just like the bear joke, running is really the best defense. Usually all that means is to build stamina. We can start with some good brisk walks, work up to jogging, and then work on running for speed for short distances. Then we can work on agility."

She gave him a small smile, which was a great sight. "I guess I can do that. Already I have to nearly jog just to keep up to you when you're walking."

He smiled back. "There you go. We can start with that. We won't jog or run until you can do a fast walk and not get out of breath, and we can do that at the park. I hear tomorrow is going to be good weather."

She nodded. "Okay. That sounds good." She inhaled deeply and then checked her watch. "Let's get that duct tape you need and then I need to call it a day."

"I can get the tape another time. Let's just go."

He tried to walk slowly through the mall so they could spend more time together, but too soon, they reached the door.

Since she was obviously still nervous about being alone, Cory turned with her instead of going to his pickup truck, which was on the other side of the lot.

"What are you doing?" she asked when he stepped off the curb beside her.

"I'm going to walk you to your car."

"You don't need to do that."

He shook his head. "Probably not, but I just want to make sure everything is okay." He'd barely finished his words and they were already at her car. "How did you get a parking spot so close to the door?"

"Just lucky I guess. I'll see you tomorrow. I'll text when I'm ready. Probably around ten?"

"Sure."

He stood, watching as she slipped into the car, started it and drove away so quickly he didn't know how she had time to do up her seat belt.

She hadn't even really said goodbye. Come to think of it, she'd obviously been nervous. Since she couldn't be nervous of a potential attack when he was with her, it hit him like a baseball bat between the eyes that she was probably still a little afraid of him.

That wasn't what he wanted. He wanted her to be comfortable with him. He wanted a relationship, which couldn't happen if she was scared or nervous in any way.

He turned and headed to his truck.

He didn't know if it would be the right thing, but he had an idea about what he could do.

Tomorrow, he'd find out if it would work.

Chapter 4

Daphne turned into the parking lot for the park and didn't know whether to cringe or smile. Cory had told her his truck would be hard to miss, and he was right.

The monstrous vehicle loomed above all else, just as he did. Big, black, with a moose face painted on the side, his 4x4 crew cab, with the big tough-treaded tires, stood taller than every other vehicle around it. Maybe even in the whole lot. And there he was, as imposing as his truck, standing beside it, leaning against the driver's door, waiting for her.

They'd talked about choosing between walking around the field that would be full of people or walking down the trail, which was wasn't as well traveled, meaning they wouldn't be in sight of another person every minute. He'd told her to think about it and let him know when she got there.

Knowing he was so understanding of her fears almost made her cry. She didn't want that. She'd already put him enough awkward situations without adding tears—besides, she'd already done that, too.

During the group therapy sessions she'd attended, things some of the other ladies shared had changed her perspective of being alone and of being with a man in a deserted location.

Only one lady in the group had been attacked by a man she hadn't known. Everyone else had been a victim or, like herself, a near-victim, of date rape, where they'd known the man who had attacked them.

Daphne wasn't sure if these confessions opened her eyes to the reality of things she'd never before considered or opened the door to unrealistic fear.

Over and over she'd told herself that Rick trusted Cory, and therefore she also needed to. He was safe.

Yet now, looking at him as surely David had faced Goliath, she didn't feel quite so confident. While it was true that David had taken Goliath to the ground with one small stone, people didn't think further along the chain of events. David's small stone hadn't killed Goliath. David had killed Goliath with Goliath's own sword.

There was no sword here. Her only means of self-defense was her purse. And if she clobbered Cory with it, it would probably wreck her cell phone.

She pulled into a spot a few spaces away from his truck, turned off the engine and got out. He waved, but didn't approach her. Instead he waited for her to come to him.

As she had, Cory had dressed casually. The weather wasn't quite warm enough for shorts, so he also wore sweatpants. Although, the only reason she'd chosen the sweatpants was that her jeans were too loose. She couldn't run if her pants were ready to fall down. The sweatpants tied around her waist with a drawstring, which was safe.

Approaching him, she cleared her throat and patted her pocket. "I decided to go on the trail. I brought my camera."

Cory's eyebrows rose. "I think it would better if we walked around the perimeter of the fields. The trail is a more scenic walk, but it's a gravel path, which makes the ground is uneven. I wanted to walk at a fast pace, not a leisurely walk. If that's what you really want we can, but I was thinking of exercise, not a nature stroll. I don't think we're going to be in any position to take pictures."

"Oh." She stopped to think, realizing he would probably be bored on the trail. "You're with nature stuff every day and probably want to spend your time with people."

"Not really. I enjoy being out in nature, nothing will change that. I was only thinking of what would be more level ground."

She didn't know how fast he wanted her to go, but regardless, he would be disappointed. "I'm not in very good shape for running. I don't know if I ever was."

"That doesn't matter. We're going to start slowly

and comfortably, and this is the place we're going to do it. The plan is to work up to some endurance."

"I guess." As she came to his side, he turned and began walking to the park, so she continued alongside him.

When they got to entrance, he stopped. "Let's start with a fast walk rather than a run. That's going to be enough of a challenge since you sit behind a desk all day." He grinned. "I know what it's like in the winter, when sometimes I'm deskbound for a week at a time."

A week. She'd been deskbound, as he called it, for about four years. "But all summer long you probably walk up and down the trails every day."

"Something like that."

Remembering how hard it had been to keep up with him at the mall, when he was walking his normal pace, she still wasn't sure this was a great idea, but it was a start.

"Okay, let's go."

At first they made small talk as they walked, but it was an embarrassingly short amount of time before she couldn't walk at the speed and talk at the same time. Then, even more humiliating, it didn't take much longer and she was gasping for air and sweating so much she thought her glasses would slip off her face.

Cory slowed his pace, looked down and smiled at her. "We're going to slow down for a while, but we can't stop. When your heart rate levels out, let me know, and we'll pick up the pace again."

For this, she could choke out a reply. "No. I can't."

His brow knotted. "Okay. But we're not stopping. We'll just slow down."

True to his word, he slowed, but his pace was still faster than comfortable, and she didn't think she could speak without gasping. To keep from embarrassing herself, she kept silent.

The third time around the field, he slowed to a pace comfortable for her. At least comfortable enough to talk. "Are we done, or do you want to go around one more time?"

He checked his watch. "I think we're done for the day. We just need to get something to drink." But he didn't turn toward the concessions. He kept walking past the food stands and headed toward the parking lot.

She followed him in silence, this time not because she couldn't talk, but because she didn't know what to say.

"I brought drinks," he said as they approached his truck. "Not because I'm too cheap to pay for them at the concession stand—even though they are outrageously priced. I brought drinks with electrolytes that we need after exercising. Especially you, because you worked up a sweat."

She didn't like a man telling her she was sweaty, but it was the truth.

He aimed his remote at the truck to unlock it, then opened the door, reached in and then handed her a bottled blue drink. "Drink this, then we can go back to the park and have an early dinner."

"I hate to tell you this, but I'm not hungry." Yet, as

the words came out of her mouth, a sensation of hunger came over her, as if just thinking about it made it happen. "Wait. I changed my mind."

He smiled. "I thought you might. We've been walking for nearly an hour, and you've been keeping up a good pace."

Maybe for herself, yes, but from what she'd seen, it had been a normal walk for Cory. Daphne didn't want to consider what he would think would be a fast pace for him, with his long legs. Today, when she'd been ready to drop, he hadn't even worked up a sweat. He'd probably even been bored, since she was unable to talk.

She finished the drink, then handed him the empty bottle. "Thanks. That was a great idea. But I'm not so sure about going back to get something to eat here, and I'm not fit to sit in a restaurant." She especially wasn't fit to sit in an enclosed vehicle with him. She needed a shower, and failing that, to stay downwind. "After all that exercise it doesn't seem right to eat any of the greasy stuff from any of the concessions."

His smile deepened. "I was hoping you'd say that. Do you like chicken?"

Before she could answer, he reached back into the truck and brought out a tote bag.

"You brought supper?"

He nodded. "Yup. Don't think I went to a lot of work. It's all bought. All I did was put it together." He reached behind the seat again, this time bringing out a bag that she could tell from the sound contained plates and cutlery. "It's still early so we should get a nice picnic table. If not I have a blanket so we can sit on the ground."

She hadn't been on a picnic since she'd been a child. Alex had never taken her to a park; she'd never shared a meal anyplace other than a restaurant with him. "You know what… I'd like to sit on the grass. Bring the blanket."

His eyebrows scrunched. "Really? Okay. But only if you're sure."

"I'm sure."

Once more he reached behind the seat and brought out a classic and well-used gray picnic blanket. It even looked like the one her parents had used when she was a child. Only Cory's was obviously more used, so well-used that some spots were even threadbare.

This time walking at a pace comfortable for her, he led her to a grassy spot near the picnic tables. As he lifted the food containers out of the insulated tote, Daphne unpacked the plates—real glass plates and real cutlery—from the other bag.

The only disposable items were napkins.

When everything was set out and ready to be served, Cory paused to say a short, quiet prayer then began to open the containers.

Daphne couldn't hold back her smile. "I haven't been on a picnic since I was a kid. This brings back such memories. Rick and I had those high-powered pump-type water guns, I forget what they were called, and we ran all over the park hiding then squirting each other. Did you have picnics with your family when you were a kid?"

"No."

She waited for him to say more, but he lowered his head and reached into the insulated tote for more blue-colored drinks.

"When Rick invited a friend to come with us, my dad teamed up with me while my mom just sat back and shook her head. We always won. My mom says that's why Rick became a cop. Sometimes it was just me and my dad. He always let me win, but it was still fun." She stopped, smiling at more memories. "Sometimes it was me and Mom against Rick and Dad. Whenever that happened it always ended up with Mom and Dad having it out while Rick and I just watched. It was hilarious watching them squirting each other."

"I'm an only child," he mumbled, not looking up. "It was just me and my mother. My mother didn't do water fights with me, or anyone."

She didn't miss the point that he didn't say anything about his father passing away when he was young, which meant that either his father had left when Cory was very young or had never been around at all.

She waited a bit longer for him to say something, but when he didn't, she thought it best not to ask. Growing up, a number of her friends had come from blended families. Everyone she'd known whose parents had gone through a divorce saw their fathers on scheduled visits or alternating weekends. One friend disappeared all summer to live with her father then came back a week before school started.

She'd never known anyone whose father wasn't in the picture at all.

When the silence hung for an uncomfortable length of time, Daphne thought it best to change the subject. "You sure brought a lot of stuff. Even real plates and cutlery. I've never been on a picnic with real plates before."

He sighed and then looked at her. "You'll never see me using paper plates or plastic knives and forks. I do a lot of campground work in the summer, and I see too much where people leave all their garbage in the sites. Or even worse, I've seen people bring foam cups and plates and then burn them in the campfires. That's so bad for the environment. When you're out camping, you're supposed to respect nature, not burn hazardous materials and send toxic chemicals into the air."

He paused and pinched the bridge of his nose with his fingers. "Sorry. I shouldn't be ranting. I had planned to bring you here for a nice picnic. Would you like some pickles?" He opened a small jar of dills and held it toward her.

She would bet that he diligently recycled all his jars as well as the drink bottles. "Sure. I'd love some pickles."

"How are you feeling now that you're sitting down?"

Daphne sighed. "I want to say fine, but I'm not. I realize how badly out of shape I am if I can't even do a fast walk for a period of time. I should probably join a gym or something."

He smiled. "Did Rick tell you that's where we met, the gym?"

"No. He didn't." But now that she knew, it wasn't really a surprise. Rick went to the gym often, and with the shape Cory was in, it wasn't a surprise, either.

"I don't know if going to the gym would be a good idea for you right now. I know it sounds wrong, but not many people who go to the gym are really out of shape. Many newbies are already in good shape and they go either for maintenance or to go to ridiculous lengths for extreme bodybuilding. Even the women. I think right now it would be devastating to your self-confidence. I'd like to keep working with you. When you've worked up to a certain point, I know some really great trails to build up your endurance."

"I suppose there are high minimum standards for strength and endurance to do what you do, isn't there? I read that forest rangers also do search and rescue, and if it's urgent, you have to help fight forest fires, too."

"Yup."

Doing those heroic things, and not talking about how strong and heroic he was to do them, said a lot about him as a man. Although search and rescue, and especially fighting forest fires, was dangerous. Not the same as police work, but still dangerous in a different way.

By the time they were packed up and ready to leave many other people had come to also have a picnic, and had already left.

"I guess you don't want to go out for coffee or anything, do you?"

She shook her head. "No. I just want to go home and have a shower and go to bed. I'm really tired, which is another reminder of how badly out of shape I am."

"What about tomorrow morning? Are you going to church? I'd like to go with you."

At the thought of going to church, her blood went cold. "No. I haven't been to church since...well, you know. I went once and everyone kept asking about Alex. I haven't told anyone except my pastor all the details about what happened. Everyone is blaming me for him moving away so fast, and they're all talking, conjecturing what I've done to drive him away. I can't face them. I can't talk about it. I won't. I haven't been back since."

Cory's brows knotted. "How about if you come with me to my church? You don't know anyone there and you don't have to say anything you don't want to."

A million thoughts coursed through her. She couldn't say she was alone and that God had abandoned her. At the last second, literally, Rick had showed up to save her from the final invasion. She couldn't blame God for Alex's actions—she could only blame Alex. But she should have thanked God for Rick coming when he had, and she hadn't.

Now she had one more person, not a paid therapist, but a friend, even if he was a friend of her brother's, who wanted to help. Maybe he could still be her friend when she got herself together again.

She'd already told herself it was time to get her life together, and to get back in touch with people. It looked as if it was time to get back in touch with God, too.

Daphne cleared her throat. "Sure. I can do that. Give me the address and I'll meet you there."

He opened his mouth and raised one finger in the air but didn't speak. He lowered his finger. "Sure. I'll text it to you." He reached into his pocket for his phone and started texting. Soon her phone sang out the text ringtone.

"Great," she said, trying to mean it. "I'll see you tomorrow morning."

Again, Cory found himself waiting in a parking lot for Daphne.

Usually by this time Sunday mornings he was already inside, greeting people and handing out bulletins.

Today, he smiled and nodded at everyone as they passed by him on their way to the building while he leaned against his truck, his ankles crossed, trying to look casual, when he was anything but. He was starting to get nervous that Daphne wasn't coming.

Her home church should have been the first place she'd go for help and support, but he did understand why she hadn't gone back. Hopefully she could find the same support here that he had received when he'd needed it. But he also knew that first she was going to feel awkward in a crowd of strangers.

Not that his church was exactly a crowd. It was a

comfortable enough group that everyone knew everyone else, even if just by name. Cory checked his watch, then reached for his cell phone so he could text her. The same second he laid his hand on his phone, her car came into the lot.

He smiled like a kid in the candy store as he watched her circle, trying to get a spot closest to the door of the building.

As she exited her car and approached him, he pushed himself to a standing position.

"Hi. I was getting worried."

Her cheeks turned pink, which he thought was a good sign. "Sorry. I'm kind of embarrassed about the reason I was nearly late."

"It's okay. You're here now."

The pink turned to red. "I feel like I have to tell you. It sounds so dumb, but I couldn't find anything to wear. You said it was casual so I wanted to wear jeans, but everything I picked looked sloppy because it was a couple of sizes too big. You're right. I do need to gain the weight back. I don't know many women who would say that, but I'm going to be honest. I really looked at myself, and don't feel comfortable."

He extended one arm toward her, then quickly withdrew it and rammed his hand into his pocket. As much as he wanted her to hold his hand, that wasn't going to happen right now. Maybe one day, but not today.

"Then after church I'll take you out for something fattening. You can make all the women around you jealous as you eat the whole thing and enjoy it. We'd better go in. There will be lots of good seats, but I don't like to rush."

As they entered the foyer, Cory had to smile when he saw his friend Dave handing out bulletins. He'd never seen Dave do anything so outgoing before. Not that Dave was shy, but he didn't interact with people very much.

The second Dave saw Daphne he looked back and forth between the two of them and his eyes widened. He stiffened then smiled graciously, not doing a very good job of hiding his surprise that for the first time, ever, Cory had brought a woman to church.

Dave extended one hand toward Daphne. "Welcome to St. Nick's. I see you're with Cory. I'm Dave. And you are?"

Cory sighed. "Dave, meet Daphne."

As he spoke Dave's name, Dave's wife, who had been talking with a group of women, turned her head. The second she laid eyes on Daphne she excused herself and joined them.

"Hi. I'm Ashley. I'm with him. And I can see you're with Cory."

Daphne wasn't as with him as Ashley was with Dave, but if he had his way, that would change as quickly as possible.

Daphne smiled hesitantly. "Hi."

When she didn't say more, he tugged a bulletin out of Dave's hand. "I'm going to have to give you lessons at handing out bulletins. You're supposed to let go when someone wants one."

While Dave's jaw dropped, Ashley started laughing.

Cory led Daphne toward the sanctuary, but didn't get very far. Another friend, Jeff, was almost jogging toward him, probably to check out the woman he'd brought. His wife Natasha wasn't very far behind. No doubt both of them wanted to check out the reason he wasn't handing out bulletins this week.

Before he had a chance to warn Daphne, Jeff and Natasha were standing in front of them.

Natasha smiled warmly. "Hi. Welcome to St. Nick's. I see you're with Cory."

Cory cleared his throat. "You're the second person who's said that. Yes, we're together. Duh."

Jeff grinned ear to ear. "I just wanted to be introduced to the reason Dave's handing out bulletins." Jeff leaned closer to him and lowered his voice. "He's not very good at it, you know." He turned back to Daphne. "I'm Jeff, and this is my wife, Natasha."

Again, Daphne smiled hesitantly. "Hi," she said, barely audible.

Cory very visibly checked his watch. "I don't mean to be rude, but we need to find a seat. We'll catch you later, after the service."

Daphne looked around then spoke, lowering her voice. "Jeff is right. Dave seemed a bit awkward about handing out bulletins, as though he's never done it before."

Busted. "You nailed it. It is Dave's first time handing out the bulletins. I usually do it, but today he's doing it for me. It's a good job. You get to say hello to everyone, then you don't have to worry about being pulled into a long conversation. Each conversation only lasts as long as it takes for the next person to walk in the door."

"I've never thought of it that way before. At my church there are usually about five hundred people attending the service, so the people who hand out bulletins really don't talk. They just give everyone a quick greeting as people shuffle past and continue on their way."

"Speaking of being on our way, we really should go sit down. Since the congregation is small everyone usually scrambles in at the last minute before the service starts. Let's get a good seat while everyone is still out in the lobby." Not that there was ever a bad seat here.

Since every other Sunday he talked to everyone as they came in, now that he wasn't talking, everyone was looking at him. He didn't know if it was because everyone missed the conversation or curiosity since for the first time he'd brought a woman with him.

Hopefully she'd come again with him next week, and the week after, and they'd just get to know her a bit without being overwhelming.

As they sat, Daphne looked around, up at the small podium to the simple wooden cross on the wall.

"You were right. This place is quite small, but in a good way. Everyone seems very friendly."

"Yeah. They are." Sometimes a little too friendly, but he couldn't consider that to be bad.

Her voice lowered to a whisper. "What is that thing?"

"It's an overhead projector. That's what churches

used to use to project the words for the songs before PowerPoint. Pastor Rob doesn't see the need to buy anything new until the old one goes."

"It's held together with duct tape. Just barely."

Dave smacked himself on the forehead. "Now I remember what I needed the duct tape for." He lowered his hand. "Although, if that last bit cracks without the tape, maybe finally Pastor Rob will have to move forward with technology."

As Daphne smiled, Pastor Rob stepped up to the microphone and welcomed everyone to the service.

Cory tried to pay less attention to Daphne and more to the pastor's words. But he couldn't help noticing that she knew most of the worship songs and, even better, she appeared to be paying rapt attention to the sermon. Overall, she seemed to be enjoying the service.

Cory sat back and smiled.

If things went well, she'd enjoy his plans for after the service even more.

Chapter 5

When the pastor gave his final blessing, Daphne found herself surprised to be disappointed that the service was over. Usually, like the rest of the crowd at her home church, she started to feel fidgety ten minutes before the sermon was over; longer if the pastor went overtime

Here, the pastor finished at twelve noon on the dot.

She wanted him to speak longer.

She turned to Cory. "Is it always like this?"

One eyebrow quirked. "What do you mean? The time? Yeah, Pastor Rob is usually finished right at noon."

Daphne shook her head. "No. Not just that. All through the sermon people kept interrupting your pastor. Asking questions and making comments. Like it was normal."

"Uh… Isn't it normal?"

She wanted to tell him that it wasn't, but he looked so comfortable here, she didn't want to burst his bubble. "How long have you been attending here?"

"I don't know. A few years, I guess."

"Have you ever gone anywhere else?"

"Not really."

She couldn't help but blink. "Are you saying this is the first church you've ever been to?"

"Kinda. Yeah."

Daphne forced herself to keep looking into his eyes instead of looking around the building. Relying on memory, she recapped the place.

It was an old building in an older neighborhood. To say there was nothing fancy here was an understatement. Cory had told her to dress casually, and this place defined casual as no church she'd ever been to. In setting, in mood and in the pastor's presentation. In the middle of the city, it felt like a visit with grandma down on the farm.

It was simple to a fault. But it worked.

Cory's voice broke her out of her mental meanderings. "How would you like to go for lunch? There's a great place a few blocks away. My friends are coming this way, and I know they'll be hungry."

Sure enough, the people he'd introduced her to earlier appeared beside them.

Daphne stood, but Cory remained seated.

Jeff spoke first. "If you've got nothing better to do, we're going to have lunch at a little bistro a few blocks away. Would you two like to come with us?

They have great bacon cheeseburgers with a special sauce that will make you think you died and went to heaven." He paused and looked toward the front, at the wooden cross on the wall. "Am I allowed to say that in church?"

His wife poked him then turned to smile at Daphne. "They have lots of great things, not all with bacon."

Jeff's cheeks turned red and Natasha bit back a grin, making Daphne wish she knew the joke.

Beside Natasha, Ashley smiled. "If there're six of us we can still fit in the little private alcove booth in the corner. We have a standing reservation for it every Sunday."

Daphne's first reaction was to decline and say she needed to go home, but she held back her reply. She'd told herself that she needed to start going out again, and this was a good way—a casual setting in a relaxed atmosphere.

Aside from the fact that it was obviously three couples, when she and Cory were not a couple. But since they were together, that would be their assumption. They had no way of knowing that Cory was only a friend of her brother, helping her get back on her feet.

Daphne turned to Cory, who was still seated. "I think a bacon cheeseburger sounds good. What about you?"

Jeff made a fist pump in the air. "Yes!"

Natasha turned sideways to give her husband a dirty look, then turned and smiled at Daphne. "Don't mind him. He goes a little crazy when someone mentions bacon." She lowered her voice. "It's his comfort food, like women use chocolate. He ate a lot of bacon before we were married." She covered her stomach with one hand and grinned. "It's a good thing I don't gain weight easily."

Cory stood. "That sounds good. I'd love to grab a burger. We'll meet you there."

When his friends were out of earshot, Cory turned to her. "It's only a few blocks away, but it doesn't have a parking lot. Whenever I join them, rather than try to find a big enough parking spot on the street I leave my truck here and walk. So that leaves us two options. Three, actually. You can drive and meet me there, we can both walk or we can both go in your car."

She pictured the tight fit. "Would you squeeze yourself into my little car again?"

Cory shrugged his shoulders. "Sure."

She looked down at her feet—her sneakered feet—and shrugged her shoulders. "I dressed casual like you said, and I need to get more in shape, so let's walk."

This time he walked at a pace comfortable for her, which gave her a chance to ask a few more questions about his church. Much too soon, they arrived at their destination.

She followed him inside to join his friends, already seated. The oddly configured room had one large booth in a recessed corner, which sequestered it away from the other four tables in the small room. Apparently the majority of the business was take-out.

Daphne tried not to look surprised to see both ladies sitting on one side of the table and the two men on the other.

Ashley patted the empty seat at the end of the bench of what was apparently the ladies' side. "Sit here. We decided that this was the best way for six of us."

As Daphne and Cory slid in, Natasha rested her elbows on the table, linked her fingers, then leaned forward and rested her chin on the cradle her fingers made. With a dreamy sigh, she looked across the table at Jeff. "This way we can look at each other. Isn't it kind of silly when couples sit beside each other when they go out? Then you can't really see each other properly."

While Natasha looked across the table at Jeff, Jeff leaned toward Natasha, something like in *Lady and the Tramp* before they shared the spaghetti. Just as all Natasha's attention was glued to Jeff, all Jeff's attention was glued to Natasha.

Daphne looked across the table at Cory, who was staring at Jeff as if he'd lost his mind.

A man poked his head out from the window to the drive-thru area. "Four usuals?" When he saw six of them, his eyes widened. He cleared his throat, stepped out and approached them. "Sorry. What can I get for you folks?"

Daphne looked up at the menu board, although she didn't know why. She already knew what she wanted. "A bacon cheeseburger platter, please, with coffee."

The man put his notepad back in his pocket without writing anything down. "And for you, same thing, super-sized, with gravy on the fries. Right?"

At Cory's nod, the man turned his head toward the kitchen. "Anita! Make that six number eights for table five! One super-sized with a side of gravy!"

After the man returned to the kitchen, Daphne didn't contribute much to the conversation, but she did enjoy watching Cory's friends. They all had fun being together, and when they saw she didn't really feel like talking, they respected her preference not to say much and included her without asking questions.

Being with them showed her the kinds of things she should have looked for in a relationship—few of which she'd had in the relationship with Alex, now that she thought about it. What impressed her the most was that even though nothing serious was being discussed, she could see the capitulation, or sometimes negotiation, before they moved on to the next topic.

Until the meals came and Natasha reached for the ketchup.

"Hey!" Jeff reached forward and covered Natasha's hand with his, freezing the ketchup bottle between them. "You always get the ketchup first. It's my turn."

"Ladies first," Natasha retorted then stuck out her tongue at him.

"I need to test it first to see if it's the brand you like, or the kind I like."

"The kind you like has too much sugar, and the store brand is cheaper."

While they continued to debate various ketchup issues, Dave reached between them and grabbed the bottle. At his touch, both let go but kept bantering. Dave extended the bottle toward Ashley. "Here. While they fight over it, you take it."

Ashley shook her head. "No, you always give it to me first. This time you use it first."

Dave extended it further toward her. "No, I had it first last time. It's your turn."

Cory let out a breath of air. "Oh, for crying out loud," he muttered, taking the bottle from Dave's hand, since Ashley still hadn't. "You two are worse than Chip and Dale. Here," he said as he held it out toward Daphne. "Your fries are going to get cold by the time they decide who gets it first. You take it."

Daphne looked at the bottle. Automatically she almost told him to use it first since it was in his hand, but he had gravy with his fries and didn't need it.

"Thanks…" she muttered as she accepted it. As she dotted ketchup onto her fries she watched the other two couples as they continued to banter, completely ignoring their meals. All of them looked as if they were trying not to laugh, yet no one gave up.

That kind of thing had never happened with Alex. She'd always given in to whatever he'd wanted because he had always been so serious. They'd never had play fights and now that Daphne thought about it, they'd never had a real fight, either. Alex had simply expected that everything would be the way he deemed best and, not wanting to make issues, Daphne had always given in before anything had escalated. Until the first time she'd told him no—and that had changed her life.

It was the kind of person she was. She gave in too easily most of the time.

Today, that was going to stop.

Finally the ketchup bottle got passed around, and they shared stories of favorite books and movies as they ate.

When it was time to leave, they found themselves standing in a group at the door, ready to go their separate ways.

Jeff and Natasha whispered between the two of them and then Jeff turned to everyone else. "If no one has anything better to do, you're all welcome to come over to our place for the afternoon."

Dave and Ashley looked at each other, then turned back to Jeff. "Sure, we'd like that," Dave said.

Cory looked toward Daphne. "I'm okay with that if you are."

She didn't know him well, but earlier she'd heard Jeff talking about a new barbecue with some exciting new features he wanted Cory to look at, so it didn't take a rocket scientist to figure out what Cory preferred.

If this was the time to see what he would do, she knew what she had to do.

She turned to Jeff. "Not this time, if you don't mind." She let her words hang, and held her breath.

Cory shrugged his shoulders. "Okay, maybe next week, if I don't see you sooner. Have fun. Catch you later." Before more words were exchanged, he turned back to Daphne. She quickly said her goodbyes and they began walking back to the church parking lot.

She didn't say anything, waiting for him to question why she'd declined the invitation knowing he wanted to go.

As they walked he checked his watch. "What would you like to do for the rest of the afternoon? Anything in particular? The day is still young."

The words were out before she could stop them. "If you want to go back with your friends, I'll just go home."

"I'd rather spend the day with you. I can see Jeff's barbecue anytime."

"Okay." Except she really hadn't thought about doing anything for the day. She'd really planned to go home after church, but had been sidelined by the lunch invitation. "How about if we go to the park for a walk?"

He turned to her and smiled. "We were just there yesterday, but if that's what you want, sure."

She waited for him to make another suggestion about going somewhere else, but he didn't. On the positive side, being Sunday afternoon, the park was likely to be much more crowded than the day before. "How about if we go on the nature walk this time?"

He nodded. "Sure."

As they walked, he talked about the various species of squirrels and some of the varieties of birds they would see.

"We should take both vehicles," he said when they reached the church parking lot. "It would be silly to have to come back later."

"I agree. I'll see you there."

She noticed that he followed her the whole way to the park. It felt strange to have the monstrous black pickup behind her. If they'd had something to make a ramp, she probably could have parked her car in the back of his truck and still closed the tailgate.

Just as she pulled into the parking lot, her phone sang out that Rick was calling.

She quickly pulled into a parking spot and answered.

"Hey, I was getting worried about you. You've been out all day. Is everything okay?"

"Yes," she replied without hesitation. "After church I went out for lunch with Cory and his friends, and now we're going for a walk at the park."

"Really?"

"Yes. Rick, I'm okay. Really."

"Okay. Just don't be too late."

"I won't be. Thanks for calling."

Getting out of her car, she realized she did feel okay. Not one hundred percent okay, but more okay than she'd felt in a long time.

Hopefully, at least for the rest of the day, it would stay that way.

With his big truck following Daphne's small car, Cory felt like an elephant trailing a mouse. But since she'd brought her own car, this was the only way to make sure she got home safely.

After the park they'd toured the Seattle Aquarium and given it wasn't summer hours yet, the aquarium closed at 6:00 p.m. Since they'd been walking all day, both of them had worked up an appetite, so they'd gone for a late dinner and ended up doing more talking than eating, which was a lot.

Her brother had called a number of times to make sure she was okay. Despite her assurances, Rick didn't stop calling until Cory took the phone and told Rick to quit worrying, that he would escort Daphne home to make sure she was safe.

Then they'd lost track of the time.

Now it was nearly ten.

Sure enough, when they pulled up in front of the house, Rick was standing on the porch, his arms crossed, looking every inch an annoyed cop, even out of uniform.

It was time to face the music.

Cory climbed out of his truck at the same time as Daphne got out of her car. When she walked toward Rick, Rick's expression tightened. "I expected you to be back at least before dark," Rick snapped before Daphne had barely opened her mouth. He then turned to glare at Cory.

Daphne reached forward and rested her hand on Rick's arm. "This is my fault, not Cory's. Don't be mad at him."

Rick stiffened even more. "The last time I talked to either of you, Cory said he'd have you home 'shortly,'" he said, adding a sarcastic emphasis to the word. "That was two and a half hours ago."

Even though Rick's anger was unreasonable, it was probably justified considering her history. Therefore, Cory needed to deal with this right now, before it got any worse. But he couldn't say what he wanted to in front of Daphne.

He turned to her. "It's okay. But I think Rick and I need to have a man-to-man."

She looked up at him. He wasn't sure how to read her expression, but it looked as if she thought he was a few turnips short of a full load.

He nodded once to show her he had everything under control. She turned and slowly made her way into the house, looking over her shoulder at him a few times before she made it all the way to the door.

The second the door closed behind her, Rick narrowed his eyes. "I know I asked you to take her out, but I only meant once. There's stuff you don't know. Important stuff."

Cory leaned back against the post for the porch and stuck his hands into his pockets, wanting to take the least intimidating stance possible while Rick acted like a protective mother bear. "She told me. I do know."

Rick's eyes narrowed as he glared at Cory. "What do you know?"

"About the night with Alex. What happened. And how you got there at the last possible second and stopped him."

Cory could almost see the thoughts running through Rick's head. First the shock that Daphne had told him, then his face tightened, probably reliving the vision of breaking into the car to save his sister, and then a sudden sobering as though he was trying, too late, to hide how he felt.

Rick sighed and his whole body sagged. "I don't know what to say. I can't believe she told you. She hasn't told anyone. Not even her best friend, or at least who used to be her best friend, because her best friend is, or rather, was Alex's sister."

"I know." Cory nodded. "She says everyone thinks it's her fault that Alex moved away so fast. When she started to give a few hints of what happened they accused her of lying, so she didn't say any more. I know she's completely broken off contact with everyone. That's one reason why I took her to my church this morning. So she could meet some new people in a safe environment."

Rick turned, not looking at Cory as he spoke. "Over the past week or so she's been talking about starting to get out again. She hasn't talked about dating, but she has said that when she does, she'll be looking for a geek-type guy who's short and skinny and wears glasses."

Cory gulped. Pretty much the opposite of him, which was probably why Rick had told him. But as far as subtle hints went, he wasn't taking it. "I'd still like to keep seeing her, if she'd like to keep seeing me. We talked about joining a swim club together on Tuesday nights."

"Why?"

Cory tried to look relaxed, but the tension in him shot to levels like the last time he'd come face to face with a cougar that had been backed into a corner. He didn't think this was a good time to tell Rick that he was falling in love with his sister.

He shrugged his shoulders. "We could both use the exercise."

Rick's eyes narrowed. "Really?"

"Yeah. Swimming is great exercise. Cheap, too."

"Are you kidding me?"

"I think Daphne would have fun. It's with people, but you don't really need to talk to anyone. Like going to the mall, except it is good exercise."

"Why all this talk about exercise? Daphne doesn't need to lose weight. The opposite, she's a little thin."

"She needs to gain some strength, and she wants to build herself up a bit. As much as possible, anyway."

"Why with you? You're twice her size. At least."

Cory didn't need a reminder of that. "I don't know. I'm only glad she wants to go with me. I..." This was really not the time to say how his feelings for her were growing every day. "...like swimming." Aside from the fact that he couldn't remember the last time he'd been in a chlorinated pool, which meant it had been many years.

Rick glanced to the door, turned back to Cory and spoke barely above a whisper. "I'm not sure that's a good idea. I don't know how well she can see without her glasses."

Not being able to see wasn't something he'd considered. He didn't know what it was like to need corrective lenses. His own vision was 20/20.

"It can't be too bad, or she wouldn't have agreed. Can it?"

"I don't know. It's not something we've ever talked about."

"She won't have to read. All she has to do is go in a straight line, and there will probably be lane markers. I can't imagine it would be that bad."

Even though it was obvious she wore glasses, Cory had never considered that the lack of good vision without them might hinder her efforts to defend herself.

Now he had something else to consider when she needed to try to rebuild her self-confidence and be able to keep herself safe. Regardless, they could still have some fun at the pool. "I'll take good care of her. Besides, the Queen Ann pool is a safe and non-threatening environment."

Rick rammed his hands into his pockets. "I'm just saying…I know my sister. She hasn't been out with people for a while, and she's always been a little shy. She tends to get lost in a crowd. For the past six months, except for her job, it's been just her and me, or she stays home with our parents when they're home."

"There's nothing she needs to be afraid of when I'm around."

"But you won't be there all the time. What then?"

Cory didn't know, but he planned to work on that. "I'll just have to see how it goes. I'll let you know."

After he told Daphne about his idea, Cory hoped he'd be sharing good news.

Chapter 6

Daphne sagged as she sat on the damp bench and looked down at her feet. It had been hard enough to put her socks on, but now she didn't know how she was going to double the effort to get her feet into her sneakers.

She couldn't remember the last time she'd been to a public pool. Aside from being so tired, she didn't know why she hadn't gone back sooner.

Cory was probably pacing the foyer right now; impatient that she was taking so long to get dressed. He probably wouldn't care if she was barefoot and her T-shirt was inside out, as long as she came out.

Just to be sure, she looked at her shirt and ran her hand down the front. The drawing of the cute puppy with the big eyes looked back at her, upside down, so everything was good.

If she could get up.

The longer she took, the worse it would be.

She pushed herself up, rolled her wet bathing suit into her towel, rammed it into her backpack and made her way out.

She found Cory standing in front of the vending machine.

"Hi," she said softly as she approached him. She opened her mouth to apologize for taking so long, but snapped it shut. Saying sorry would be a reminder that she'd been at fault and add fuel to the fire.

"Hi," he mumbled, not even turning to look at her. "I can't decide between that big chocolate-chip cookie and this chocolate bar. Which would you pick?"

"The chocolate bar," she replied without hesitation.

His finger hovered between the two buttons. He picked the chocolate bar. When it landed in the slot, he put more money into the machine and also bought the cookie. "Here, you take the chocolate bar. I changed my mind."

He'd opened the cookie wrapper and taken a bite before she'd even started peeling the paper back from the bar. All she could do was stare at him. He hadn't said a word about how long it had taken her to change. Not only was he not angry, he didn't even seem to care.

"Why are you looking at me like that?" he said between bites. "I'm hungry."

Not only was he not angry, now he looked apologetic.

She turned and meticulously began to unwrap the

chocolate bar, not wanting him to look at her while she tried to figure him out. "I have never seen anyone eat as much as you. It's a wonder you don't weigh two hundred pounds."

He laughed, causing her to look up at him. He took another bite of the cookie and grinned. "I hate to tell you this, but I weigh a good bit over two hundred pounds."

Daphne looked up. Way up. Actually, for his height, if he weighed "only" two hundred pounds, he would be thin. And he definitely wasn't thin. Now that she'd seen him in a bathing suit, in all his masculine glory, she'd witnessed firsthand that while he wasn't thin, he definitely didn't have an ounce of fat on him. Everything was solid muscle, including his six-pack abs.

And, as he'd claimed at Brad and Kayla's wedding, he did have nice legs.

If he didn't have such a gentle nature, he would have been scary.

Yet, even without knowing him, none of the other women in the pool had been scared of him. It had seemed as if every female past the age of puberty had at some point ogled him. A gray-haired elderly lady at least eighty years old had whistled at him.

He hadn't even noticed.

At the sound of an excited scream, both of them turned to watch the activity in the pool. A young boy had just launched himself off the rope swing and was now yelling and flailing his arms and legs. Seconds before he hit the water, he stopped yelling and sucked in a deep breath, stiffened and raised his arms over his head, and transformed into a beautiful dive, smoothly going into the water.

Cory ate the last bite of the cookie then threw the wrapper in the nearby wastebasket. "That's what I wanted to do. Look at how he entered the water."

"That's because he's a skinny little twerp. As you just told me, you're more than double his size and weight." She turned to look at him, while he continued to watch the lineup for the rope swing. "I couldn't believe my eyes, watching you behave like Tarzan on that thing."

Not only that, about half the people in the pool had stopped what they were doing to watch Cory sail through the air, every time his turn came up. He swung out farther than anyone else, probably because his weight gave him more momentum. Then, because of his strength, he didn't let go until the rope was almost ready to start swinging back. His entry into the water was never graceful and always with a big splash, yet it was obvious he was having fun.

Until he'd landed with a cannonball that splashed one of the lifeguards. Then he was politely asked to not use the rope swing again.

"I never came here as a kid, so I have to make up for lost time."

She couldn't imagine him as a kid.

She especially couldn't imagine what his mother must have needed to do to feed him.

"Why not? I thought you grew up in Seattle, too."

"I did. Just not this part of Seattle." He pressed his

now-free hand over his stomach. "I'm hungry. What about you? Can we go for a snack? I know this great place not far from here."

She had a feeling he knew a lot of great places. "I guess so."

"In fact, we can walk. It's—"

"No!" She held up one hand before he could say anything more. "I'm not walking. I want to sit. Relax. Enjoy myself."

"Oh."

"We can drive."

"There's not much parking. It would be best to take one vehicle and leave the other one here."

Again she looked up at him. Her first thought was to take her car, but he'd been so good to her, she didn't want to force him to squeeze into her compact economy car again.

She swallowed hard. "We can take your truck." She paused, not sure if she was telling herself she was doing the right thing or to give Cory a few seconds to process the shock.

She cleared her throat. "Now. Before I change my mind."

It wasn't as though he'd never had a woman ride in his truck before, but when he hit the remote to unlock it as they approached, he felt lost—and this time he had no compass to guide him in the right direction. Except for being with her brother, this was the first time she was going to be inside a vehicle with a man since the man she should have trusted the most had done the worst thing a man could do to a woman. It was a step she had to take, and she was doing it with him.

Now, he needed to do the right thing. He just didn't know what that would be.

He walked to the passenger door, opened it for her and waited. With the height of the running board and her short legs, he didn't know how she was going to get up. When he'd bought the truck there had been an option for an extended step but he hadn't taken it. Now he wished he had.

Cory extended one hand. "Do you need help getting up? A boost?"

"No." She shied away from him. "Please don't touch me."

"Okay." Lowering his hand, he quickly stepped back. He watched helplessly while she grabbed the back of the seat then struggled to balance enough to climb up. She really could have used a boost, but right now, if he touched her, being behind her as she crawled up, he'd probably come out of the situation with a broken nose.

Except for being a little big, he liked his nose the way it was.

His stomach flipped as she started to lose her grip. He stepped forward, willing to take the risk of getting kicked in the face, but at the last second she regained her balance and clambered up, poised awkwardly on the seat with her legs hanging down like a fish flopping out of water.

As soon as she was still, with her stomach pressed

on the seat and her feet braced at the bottom, she turned her head to look at him. "See? I made it."

"I knew you could do it." As the words came out of his mouth he hoped a bolt of lightning wouldn't strike him dead. Watching her in that awkward position, he didn't want to think of her getting into his truck if she were wearing a dress. On the way home he would stop in at a lumber yard and build her a step block that he could put behind the seat.

Getting out shouldn't be as bad. He hoped.

When she had set herself upright and was seated properly, he pushed the door closed and ran around to the driver's side.

She didn't fasten her seat belt until after he'd fastened his. The second he started the motor, she pushed the button to lower the window.

He made sure not to make any sudden moves, just as when he came across an injured or distressed animal.

"We'll be there in a couple of minutes. It's only a few blocks."

She turned and gave him a very forced smile that was so tight he wondered if it hurt. "It's okay."

It was probably the longest four minutes in history by the time he parked. At least they hadn't caught a red light.

He sat with his hand on the key as she pushed the button to roll up the window. The second it was up, he shut the motor off and got out, giving her as much time as she needed to slide out.

He stood back until her toes finally touched the ground.

"Are you okay?"

She gave him a shaky smile. "Yeah. I am. Thank you for being so understanding."

He shrugged his shoulders. "It's not a big deal." At least it wasn't to him. But he couldn't imagine being so scared of anything that it would disrupt his life and relationships with others the way it had Daphne's.

"There shouldn't be many people in there at this hour. We should get served quickly."

Daphne nodded. "We can't be too long. I don't want my car to get towed when I'm not there."

"It won't be. But we both have to be up early for work tomorrow, so we shouldn't be too long."

Sure enough, once inside they were seated immediately, and placed their orders. Once the server was out of earshot, Cory cleared his throat. "How were you today at the pool? I mean, without your glasses on. I never asked how well you can see without them. You seemed to be doing fine, but I don't really know."

"I can't read without them, and I lose details. In an emergency I could probably still drive, and I certainly don't bump into things. Why do you ask?"

"I was just wondering what would happen if you lost your glasses, how much you could see."

"Did that answer your question?"

"Yes." But not really. His real question was about how helpless she would be, and the answer was that she wouldn't be totally helpless, but her vision was impaired. Sometimes the details were important—

especially when trying to provide a description to the police.

He reached into his pocket. "I brought this for you, in case you ever need it."

He put the can on the table and waited.

She picked it up. "Bear spray? Isn't this illegal?"

Cory grinned. "Nope. In some states it's restricted, but here in Washington it's not restricted for personal protection for those over the age of eighteen."

Daphne shook it to feel the weight. "But I don't walk anywhere alone at night."

"It's not just for walking alone in bad neighborhoods in the middle of the night. Lots of women have it for any time they are walking anywhere alone, including if you work late and you're going through the parking lot alone in the dark."

She stared at the can. "Where did you get this? This is hard to get."

He gave her a weak smile. "I work where there're bears. It's regular stock. I bought it from the supplier. I got you the small size. The can I carry sometimes is pretty big."

Her face paled. "Have you ever had a bear try to attack you? Have you ever used it?"

Cory shook his head. "No. If you treat bears with respect and don't encroach on their territory, they're okay. The problems are when they get too used to people, or worse, when people leave food out for them."

She stared at the can and began to read the warning label. "This is bad stuff."

"I know. But it's not going to cause permanent injury. Usually all you have to do is aim it and a potential attacker will back off. Which means, if you're ever in a situation that you might need it, it's got to be handy. You can't tell someone to wait while you dig it out of your purse, like I've seen you do with your cell phone. You have to either have it already in your hand, or in an outside pocket of your purse, when you can reach your purse in seconds. Otherwise it's not going to do you any good."

"Thank you. I don't know what to say. I feel better already."

He didn't want to say that for her situation it wouldn't have done any good, being a date-rape situation where she knew and trusted the guy. It was only meant to improve her confidence, which right now, was the biggest hurdle.

She reached for her purse, opened it and put the can inside. "This is great, except I don't have an outside pocket on my purse. So you know what that means."

She looked up at him and smiled. The first really joyful smile he'd seen since he'd started seeing her again. Her beautiful eyes lit up, showing mix of browns like different shades of chocolate. Her smile brought out a dimple in her cheek he hadn't known she had.

She jerked her head, tossing a few strands of her full-bodied hair out of her eyes, for a few seconds making it fluff behind her as though a summer wind had touched it.

Then she looked into his eyes. Really looked. As though he was the only thing in her world that mattered.

Her gorgeous smile was for him and him alone.

He nearly went into cardiac arrest.

It was difficult to speak. "No," he choked out. "I don't know. What does it mean?"

She pressed the clasp to her purse shut and patted the top of it. "It means we have to go to the mall tomorrow."

Before he could respond, the server appeared with their orders. "Here you go. I don't mean to rush you, but we close in twenty minutes. Enjoy."

Daphne kept smiling at him even after the server left, making it hard for him to think.

If only she could smile at him like that another time.

He cleared his throat. "As nice as it is to have something to help with self-defense, there are times when that won't be enough. Like when you're caught completely off guard and you don't have those two seconds it takes to get the spray out, even if it is in an outside pocket. I've been checking around, and I found a place that teaches women some basic self-defense stuff. It teaches you what to do to escape when you can't overpower."

As expected, the more he talked, the more her smile faded. "I've seen ads in the paper for stuff like that. They seem kind of scary."

"The wife of one of the other rangers teaches a session, and I talked to him about it. I've met her a few times. It's probably good because even though she's not as short as you, she's still pretty small." And, he didn't want to say it out loud, besides being short, Tyler's wife was also a little overweight and likely not a candidate for a physical fitness test. So if Allie could fend off an attacker, then Daphne could, too. "Would you like to try it out?"

"I suppose I could. It's probably a good idea. We should start eating so they can close up."

While they ate they talked about some of the antics at the pool, including Daphne scolding him for the cannonball that had gotten him kicked off the rope swing.

He left a bigger tip than usual and paid the bill, and again found himself watching Daphne struggle to get into his truck without help. This time didn't seem so awkward, which gave him hope, although he was still going to build a step for her.

More encouraging, even though she opened the window the second he turned on the motor, she wasn't so stiff. Although he still didn't reach toward the CD player. This time she had the bear spray and he didn't want to be her first victim.

Hopefully, after the self-defense classes, she wouldn't have any victims.

This time they caught the red light on the way to rec center's parking lot, and it didn't matter.

He found a parking spot where she could open the door all the way without hitting another vehicle. After she slid out of his truck, Cory walked her to her car.

After she unlocked it, she turned to him. "I don't know what to say. For the first time in six months I'm not so scared of what could happen. I feel like I'm getting back some of the control of my life."

He smiled. "Then that's great."

She stepped closer. His heart began to beat faster. "Thank you."

Just as he opened his mouth, intending to say that she didn't have to thank him, she shuffled forward, extended her hands slightly and rested her fingertips on his stomach.

At her touch, he froze, unsure of what to do, but terrified of doing something wrong.

Since she was right in front of him, looking down, all he could see was the top of her head, the top of the frames of her glasses, and the tip of her nose sticking forward from her hair.

Transfixed, he watched as she shuffled again until she leaned against him, with her hands pressed on his lower rib cage. Then she turned her head and pressed her cheek to his chest—right over his heart, which was pounding like a freight train.

He wanted to wrap his arms around her. To lift her up so he could hold her against his chest instead of his stomach.

He wanted to kiss her.

Instead his hands trembled as he rested his fingertips to her shoulders and lightly brushed her soft, smooth hair with his thumbs. At his touch she stiffened slightly, then relaxed and leaned against him.

He'd never been so scared in his life. But at the same time, he didn't want this moment to end.

Her hands never left his chest, never went around to his back or even to his waist. They remained on his chest, where she could push if she wanted to.

He hoped she didn't want to.

On the street, a car horn sounded and a male voice hooted through the window then yelled, "Get a room!"

In the same second Daphne lifted her hands and stepped back, not pushing him, but definitely moving away. Cory quickly raised his hands off her shoulders and rammed them into his pockets. He didn't know what to say. He certainly couldn't tell her that he loved her, so he said nothing.

Her cheeks darkened as she stepped back, not looking up at him. "I need to go home." She quickly turned around, opened her car door and slid in behind the wheel. The engine fired up as soon as the door closed and she drove away with one hand on the steering wheel, the other pulling at the seat belt.

He stood, staring at the car, until he realized she was driving away without him. He turned and ran as fast as he could to his truck and roared off to catch up.

Again, he was going to follow her home to make sure she got there safely. But now, the game had changed.

If only he knew what to do about it.

Chapter 7

As Daphne began the sequence to shut down her computer, again she looked outside. When she first got the promotion she'd relished the thought of being in an office with an outside window. Now she wasn't so sure.

At the sight of the big black pickup truck with the picture of the moose on it, waiting for her in the parking lot, her stomach churned.

Part of her was happy to see him, but part of her was terrified. Not because she was scared of him, but because she wasn't.

He'd been so gentle and understanding of her phobias she'd nearly cried in front of him, which was the last thing she wanted to happen. The first time he'd taken her out he'd helped her through a panic attack, and then he fended off another moment of panic in his truck. He couldn't see her cry again.

She'd managed to hold back her tears until she'd gotten into her car. So he wouldn't see, she'd sped off. But it hadn't taken him long, with that monster of a truck of his, to catch up to her.

Fortunately he'd waited in the truck and just watched her run inside the house instead of trying to escort her to the door. Unfortunately, though, Rick had been waiting and he'd seen her streak past him with tears streaming down her cheeks. She'd called out that nothing happened on her way past, so at least Rick knew that Cory hadn't done anything bad. But she was still shaken with everything that had happened.

She hadn't openly cried about it since the night Alex had attacked her, not even during the therapy sessions. She'd just felt numb. Last night, for the first time, everything blew to the surface. She didn't know why. It just did. Her therapist said it could happen, and apparently, she was right.

So she'd been driving, alone, bawling her eyes out, and it was the start of the release she'd needed. With Cory driving behind her, he couldn't see her, just the back of the car, yet he was close enough if she needed him. She'd felt safe to let it all out, and it had all come out, in the security and safety of her car. With a little more work and a lot of prayer, this was going to be the start of being able to move on with her life.

Yet, that was now something new that scared her. When she got her act together, and she would get it together, Cory would go back to wherever forest rangers went in their time off. Before the chamber dinner, she'd only see him when he'd had time to join her brother and his friends, which now wouldn't be often enough.

She didn't know what favor Cory owed Rick that he would help her this way, but whatever it was, one day she would thank her brother for it.

Now, Cory was out there, waiting for her.

The second the computer finished shutting down, she locked up her office and went to the parking lot to join him.

She patted her purse, maybe for the last time. "Are you ready?"

"I guess so."

"I know where I want to go. It's the same mall we were at last week."

"Fine."

"If you want, we can go to the hardware store first. That way you can get the duct tape you said you needed."

"Okay."

Some of her excitement waned. "What's the matter?"

His cheeks turned red and then the color spread to his ears. "I've never been to a store that sells purses before. But I guess it's not as bad as a store that sells… uh…you know." His cheeks turned even more red.

"It's not like you think. This store sells leather goods. That means they sell laptop cases and briefcases. Men shop there, too."

His blush faded. "I guess you can tell that I've never bought a laptop case. When I'm stuck in the office I use a desktop computer. Like at home. I don't own a laptop computer. I'm really not into that kind of thing."

"It's okay. I shouldn't take long. I have a pretty good idea of what I want. Then I have a surprise for you."

At that, he perked up. "Really?"

"My parents are away visiting some relatives, so it's just Rick and me for a few days. Since we've got the house pretty much to ourselves, I want to invite you over for supper today. It'll be just the three of us. I made lasagna for supper. Rick's supposed to put it in the oven at the right time so it will be done by the time we get home."

"That sounds great. Do we need to stop by a bakery and pick up garlic bread on the way there?"

"Already covered. I had some frozen dough. It's going into the oven at the right time. I also made a salad this morning, so everything is ready. Rick will have everything in the oven when we get there."

"I'm impressed. Let's just get that purse. I can get the duct tape another time."

He followed her to the mall, and once there, she didn't feel the need to get a spot closest to the door. Instead, she parked near the end of the row, where she could park beside Cory's truck. She didn't know if that was better or worse, so she refused to think about it any more.

They'd hadn't even gone inside the leather and luggage store when she saw the perfect purse on display in the window. Not only was it the right size and shape with multiple outside pockets, it was also the right color and, best of all, it was on sale. It was bagged and paid for in less than four minutes, something she didn't think she would ever do again.

Cory stood near the entrance, smiling, with his arms crossed. "That's the way to shop."

"Not really, but..." She paused to hug the shopping bag. "This purse is just so perfect." She had a feeling she wasn't even going to wait until she got home. Once she got to the car she would probably switch everything over.

Cory pressed one hand over his stomach. "Are you ready to go? You don't need anything else, do you? I think I hear that lasagna calling."

"I'm good to go."

There was never any guessing with Cory. If what he was thinking wasn't obvious, he simply came out and said it. She liked that about him.

He jerked one thumb over his shoulder, in the direction of her house. "Race you to your place?"

"No way. We've got to obey the speed limit." She lowered her voice, pretending to be sharing a secret. "My brother is a cop, you know." At his grin, she smiled back. "Let's just hope the traffic lights are in our favor."

They were. She'd never made it from the mall to home in such little time. Cory did miss one light that she caught green, so she beat him home by the amount of time it took to pick up the bag containing her new purse, and transfer the contents of her old purse into the new one, with the bear spray and her cell phone in the outside pockets.

She was walking to the door just as Cory got out of his truck. As she reached to open the door, it swung wide before she touched the handle.

She was about to tease Rick about being so fast, until she saw his face.

"What's wrong?" Fear ran through her in a cold wave. "Is something wrong with Mom and Dad? Did they have an accident?"

Rick shook his head. "No. They're fine. It's something else."

Rick moved back to allow her access into the house, as Cory followed behind her. The second she stepped in, in addition to the smell of the lasagna cooking, the aroma of flowers hit her.

Rick pointed to the dining room table. "Some flowers came for you today."

"Flowers? I don't…" Daphne let her voice trail off. A wave of dread worse than a few minutes ago coursed through her.

Rick turned to Cory. "At first I thought they were from you, but then I looked at the writing on the envelope. I know you write like an eight-year-old, so they're not from you."

If Daphne didn't feel so sick, she would have scolded Rick for being rude to Cory. All she could do was stare at the dining room table, at a beautiful array of mixed flowers, which included two dark red roses.

Rick turned to her. "They're from Alex, aren't they?"

The second she looked at the handwriting on the envelope, she knew it was true.

The significance of the date hit her like a clanging gong. She hadn't thought about it at work, but looking at the flowers, she thought about it now.

"Yes, they're from Alex. Today is the two-year anniversary of our first date. He sent me flowers last year, one red rose surrounded by other smaller light-colored flowers. He said it was an important day that we'd celebrate for the rest of our lives, and that he'd give me a bouquet every year, with one more rose to celebrate each year. I don't understand why he would send them to me now."

Rick walked ahead of her toward the arrangement. "Do you want me to throw them out?"

"First I'm going to read the card."

With shaking hands, she plucked the small envelope from the holder then pulled a white note from the envelope.

The two men waited while she read it, but she could have cut the silence with a knife.

When she lowered the note and stared at the flowers once again, Rick piped up.

"What did he say?"

"He said he was sorry, and that he still loves me."

Cory cleared his throat then spoke so softly she could barely hear him. "Do you still love him?"

Daphne answered without hesitation. "No."

Rick didn't wait for her to say more. "Did he say where he was, or if he's coming back?"

"No. He did say that he took a promotion, and if I can forgive him, he'd like me to move there and still marry him, but he didn't say where 'there' is. But I do know that his sister knows where he is, and she's not saying, either. She made that clear the last time she spoke to me."

Rick stiffened and crossed his arms over his chest. "You can still press charges, and then 'there' will be jail."

She didn't know what to think of that. Even though God said to forgive, the Bible didn't say that there would be no punishment for wrongs. Even if she could forgive him, which she couldn't right now, it wouldn't be against God's word to press charges and have him arrested to face the punishment for what he'd done.

But she'd heard too many horror stories about rape trials. Alex could afford a better lawyer than she could, so she didn't know if she could handle her day in court.

"I can't think about that now. Get rid of those flowers." She pressed her hand to her stomach as what happened that day replayed in an endless loop in her head. "I'm sorry, I'm not hungry anymore. You two go ahead and eat without me. I think I need to be alone."

Before she broke down in front of them, she turned to go to her bedroom, but then stopped. That's where she'd gone after Rick had brought her home from the hospital, and she didn't want to go there now.

The sanctity of her room as a haven was one more

thing Alex had destroyed for her. It now came with too many memories of the night that had nearly destroyed her life.

All she could do was stand and stare down the hall. She didn't know where to go or what to do.

Cory stepped forward. "Would you like to go for a walk? Just around the block. It might help clear your head. I remember driving past an ice-cream shop a couple of blocks away. We can go there, and you can tell me all about your favorite ice cream."

Automatically she turned her head in the direction of the ice-cream shop, even though she was inside the house. A specific destination sounded good right now and a topic of distraction even better.

"That sounds like a great idea. Let's do that, and then we can come here and I'll probably be okay to eat that lasagna. We're adults. We're allowed to have dessert first."

Walking was the therapy she needed. Cory stayed with her in silence while she rambled on. By the time they got back to the house she was hungry, even after a cone.

The two men talked more than she did, catching up from the last time they were together before Brad and Kayla's wedding.

It felt comforting listening to them argue about sports teams she knew nothing about, and then they had an interesting discussion about electric versus hybrid cars.

By the time their evening was over it was late and

way past her bed time. When they realized the time, Cory didn't linger. He said a quick goodbye and left.

After the door closed behind Cory, Rick turned to her. "How are you? Are you okay?"

"Yeah. I am. Better than I thought. I'm not even going to throw out the flowers. On the way to work I'm going to donate them to the senior's center. I'll see you tomorrow."

Rick looked toward the door, then back to her. "Are you seeing Cory again tomorrow?"

"Yes. He's going to take me to a woman's self-defense class. That should be interesting. I know what they say we're going to learn, but I can't imagine doing it."

Rick stared at her as though she'd lost her mind. Maybe she had.

Tomorrow she'd find out for sure.

Cory stared at the door to the aerobics center, not sure what he should do.

She'd missed the first class, but she'd been okay to still join because the previous week they'd only had a demonstration and hadn't physically done anything.

Before Daphne had gone inside they'd sat in the truck and watched other ladies arrive. When Daphne finally got out of the truck, the women who were in the parking lot had turned to watch. If it wasn't his imagination, and he was pretty sure it wasn't, every women who had seen him cast him a dirty look, as if he was the enemy. Of course at a woman's self-defense class, he probably was.

He wasn't used to that. In uniform, at work, he was the good guy, the one people came to when they had questions or a problem. Especially little kids who always often looked at him with stars in their eyes, as though he was Superman or something. Except of course when he got stuck with the late camping shift on weekends and had to tell the rowdy campers to quiet down or put out a campfire when the risk was high. Then he was the bad guy. Yet still everyone listened.

Now, he didn't know what to do. In a normal situation, he would have simply dropped her off and gone to do what he had planned, which was go to the hardware store and finally buy that roll of duct tape he needed. Except she hadn't looked entirely confident when she'd gone inside. So, just in case she changed her mind about the class and wanted to go back home, he decided he'd better stay.

Fortunately he'd brought a copy of the new camper's handbook that he gave out to people who requested it. Not much would have changed from the previous version, but it was still a good idea to skim through it for changes. After all, he was supposed to be the expert.

He started reading, but didn't get very far when the door to the studio opened.

A woman stood in the doorway.

Daphne.

He tossed the book onto the seat and was out of the truck running toward her before she stepped out from beneath the awning.

Her eyes widened as he stopped in front of her. Strangely, she didn't look as he'd thought she would. She didn't seem scared or even nervous. "I had a feeling you would be still out there. Allie said their volunteer didn't show up. Would you like to do it?"

"Do what?"

Daphne looked up at him, right into his eyes. "Be an attacker."

Almost as though it was happening all over again, the moment that changed his life roared through his head in fast-forward. That day, it had been like someone flipped a switch in his head and he'd lost it. He didn't have many regrets in his life, but this one was big. Even now, he still had repercussions.

Losing control had changed his life, and many lives, forever. God had pulled him out of the mire, but he couldn't test God again.

Cory cleared his throat, trying to sound calm, when he felt anything but. "I'm not so sure that would be a good idea."

Daphne's cheeks turned red. "It's okay. They have, uh, protection for you."

As her meaning dawned on him, he wondered if he could crawl into a hole somewhere. "That's not what I meant. I don't want to hurt anyone."

"It won't be like that. Allie said all that happens is that you try to grab us and we try to defend ourselves. You pretty much only have to stand there."

"And let the ladies strategically hit me."

"Something like that."

Cory looked down at her, not speaking while his

mind raced. This situation wasn't the same. He didn't have to worry about someone getting the better of him, and none of them would fight dirty. All they wanted to do was to defend themselves so they could flee.

Not only that, every one of the women he'd seen go in couldn't be much more than half his weight. There would be no need to defend himself or attack back. Literally, all he really had to do was stand there wearing protective equipment and a face mask, and let them have a go at him. Maybe he might have to try to defend himself, but there was probably little point. It sounded as if the plan for today was simply for him to be a live target.

There was no possibility of anyone here doing anything to make him angry.

This class had to be effective for Daphne—or she wouldn't go back.

"Just let me get this straight. All I need to do is stand there and let the ladies try to get at my, uh, weak points, right?"

"Pretty much. You're supposed to make a grab for everyone, and then we try to defend ourselves against you."

If all he had to was stand there and let a bunch of ladies have a go at him, then he was probably safe. "I guess so. Will I need to sign a release or something?"

"Probably. I'm so glad you're going to volunteer. I feel better now." She gulped. "Even though we're learning to defend ourselves, I still don't like the thought of another man being too close to me like that. I know it sounds ridiculous, but I almost left when I heard what we were going to do."

He forced himself to relax, trying to make it look as though it didn't matter, and that he wasn't nervous. "Okay. Let the games begin."

Chapter 8

While all the women in the room watched Cory as he walked with Allie to sign the required release forms, Daphne watched the women. A mix of awe and fear pulsed through the group as one by one they realized Cory was the man they all had to try to overcome.

Not that they had to beat him. Allie said they just needed to disable him only long enough to make their escape. She'd half joked that if he were a real attacker, hurting him would be a bonus.

One of the women turned to stare at Daphne. "Is she kidding? How would we ever be able to do anything to stop a guy like that?"

Another woman turned to the speaker. "We'll just have to work harder than we thought. Allie says it's possible to defend ourselves against anyone, if we're properly trained, or unless a man is strung out on drugs and is going berserk." The second woman also turned to Daphne. "Although I don't know how. He looks like the Incredible Hulk. Where did you find this guy?"

"He's…" She stopped, wondering what exactly he was. She really didn't know. He wasn't a boyfriend— she wasn't ready for that yet. Therefore there was only one option. The truth. "He's my brother's friend." Although, he certainly didn't act toward her like any of her brother's other friends, and she was glad for that. She wanted to think that it could be more.

The realization of what she was thinking stopped her from adding anything—she wanted more than just his friendship.

Another woman snorted. "If my brother had friends like that, I wouldn't need this class."

Something in the pit of Daphne's stomach turned to a bitter lump. He was her brother's friend, and she still needed the class. But she wasn't going to point that out to the woman just in case making such a comment required an explanation.

Cory and Allie returned, with Cory wearing some rather embarrassing protective gear painted with a red target, which probably made it even more embarrassing. As he walked he adjusted the strap to a face mask, not looking at any of the ladies while he fumbled with his large fingers.

Allie rubbed her hands together. "We're almost

ready to start. Who can tell our new member, Daphne, how to sing?"

Daphne looked at Allie, then to the other ladies. "Sing? I thought it would be best to scream. Really loud."

At her comment the entire group giggled. Allie raised one hand to silence them. "SING is an acronym for the order of things to do to defend yourself against an attacker, made popular from the movie *Miss Congeniality*."

"I remember that." But even though she struggled to remember what each letter stood for, she couldn't. She could only see Sandra Bullock's character decimating Benjamin Bratt's character while the audience at the pageant watched in shock.

One woman spoke out, not waiting to be asked. "It means solar plexus, instep, nose, groin."

At the word "groin" Cory grimaced and covered the embarrassing target, causing a resurgence of the giggling.

Allie raised her hands to once more calm the group. "We're going to concentrate on one area at a time. Attention please, we don't want to run out of time."

The group calmed while Allie continued with an explanation and a slow-motion demonstration of the most effective way to deliver a series of four blows with the most effectiveness to disable Cory.

Even though Cory was there as a live crash-test dummy, Daphne found herself cringing every time Allie demonstrated how to aim, despite the fact that

Cory was adequately protected, and that Allie didn't actually strike him.

Allie also said that she considered it a bonus for the group that Cory was so big, as this gave them more motivation to fight back with more force.

At Allie's words, Daphne almost spoke out. Just because Cory was larger than the average man didn't make him any less susceptible to feeling pain.

Yet, he was doing this for her.

When class was done, she was going to have to do something to make up for it.

For now, she had to watch all the women hit Cory in all his protected parts. If that wasn't bad enough, soon she would have to hit him, too.

As the women stomped on top of his feet, which were also covered by big pads, Allie reminded everyone that even though stilettos would hurt when properly aimed, in actual practice, they weren't that stable for a sharp, aimed blow, and statistically slipped more times than punctured.

Daphne didn't want to picture that possibility. Fortunately everyone there was wearing sneakers.

Too soon, it was her turn to try to hurt Cory.

"I don't want to do this," she whispered. "Are you okay? I noticed one woman hit you in the leg where you're not padded."

His voice came out a little muffled from behind the face mask. "I might have a bruise or two, but nothing's broken. Don't worry. Give me all you've got."

Following the instructions, when Cory made a grab for her, Daphne struck out in all the strategic places, hitting all her targets first try, earning her a round of applause from the rest of the ladies.

"Well done, especially for your first time," Allie said as she helped Daphne pull off the protective hand coverings. Allie turned to Cory. "How about you? Are you okay?"

Cory pulled off the mask and shrugged his shoulders. "Sure. I guess." He made a visual sweep of the seven ladies in the room. "Some of you pack a pretty mean elbow strike. I could imagine how that would feel if I hadn't been wearing all this padding." He smiled as he pressed one hand to his stomach, but Daphne did detect a slight wince.

Allie turned to the group of ladies. "Class dismissed. Let's give Cory a big round of applause."

His cheeks darkened as the ladies clapped, which Daphne found adorable.

As everyone went to their cars, Daphne followed Cory to his truck. It seemed every time she climbed in it was a little easier, although the wooden step he'd built helped a lot.

After she was seated he picked up the step, tucked it behind the seat, then jogged around to the driver's side and got in.

As he inserted the key into the ignition switch, she turned to him. "I'm sure you worked up quite an appetite. How would you like to go to the doughnut shop we saw on the way here? My treat."

Pressing his free hand to his stomach, he turned and smiled. "An offer I can't refuse."

She had a feeling he wouldn't.

Being a passenger, she didn't have to concentrate on traffic as they exited the parking lot, but she did watch what was happening behind them in the large side mirrors.

Most of the cars turned the same way they did. A number of them made the same second turn, then a few cars still continued to make the same sequences of turns as Cory did on the way to the doughnut shop.

She didn't know if anyone regularly came to this same place, so she couldn't know for sure if they were being followed. But from the way many of them looked at him as he walked past, before he donned all the protective gear, she had a bad feeling.

She wanted to spend time alone with Cory. She didn't want company, especially people she didn't know.

Of course, as soon as the truck turned into the doughnut shop's parking lot, the three cars that had stayed behind them did the same. The ladies from the session parked and scrambled out, with the good timing to arrive at the passenger side of Cory's truck just as he retrieved the step from behind the seat and put it down so she could get out without looking like a five-year-old.

She probably should have felt guilty about not wanting them there, but she didn't.

As the women surrounded Cory he looked around at all of them, looking at him. She couldn't help but feel sorry for him.

"We come here often," one of them piped up. "I

think we should all sit at one table, since we're all here."

"Sure…" Cory murmured, then looked at Daphne. "I guess we can do that." He answered as a statement, but his voice held a question.

"Sure," she said, agreeing out loud, the word "no" echoed inside her head. She wanted to talk to Cory, just by himself. She wanted to tell him that he didn't have to be the class crash test dummy again and get beat up just for her. A few strikes had missed the padding, so she knew he would have some bruises.

Even though she'd felt nervous at the thought of physical confrontation, and even though she would not yet be able to really defend herself effectively against another man, today had been a good start and wouldn't have been possible without Cory's prompting. As with so many things in her life, it was time to move on, and now, again, with Cory's help, she was.

She wanted, and needed, to tell him how much she appreciated him.

As everyone walked together as a group to enter the coffee shop, she positioned herself beside Cory then looked up at him as she glued herself to his side.

It almost startled her that she felt so possessive about him. But he was just…likeable. Despite his size he was gentle and kind. Or maybe it was because of his size that made him that way. That he knew his own strength was unmistakable. He didn't have to be afraid of anyone or anything. Except cougars and bears. Or at least, not really afraid. He'd already told her what he did when he came in contact with wild animals. He'd said they left him alone if he allowed them a healthy dose of respect.

She doubted these women would behave the same.

Not saying she was cured, but he was the first man since Alex that she trusted.

If only she could talk with him privately tonight, but she couldn't. The best she could do was to interact with him in the group setting.

Although this may not have been the best group for that purpose. The ladies with them weren't manhaters, but they were banded together with the primary objective of learning to take down a man, which was what the classes were for. Individually each woman would have been fairly formidable. As a group, no man would stand a chance.

While everyone ordered coffee and a doughnut or muffin, she kept right with him.

Staying beside him while they selected a table, she quickly slid into the chair next to the one he selected for himself.

Joyce, one of the older ladies, selected the chair directly across the table from him. When everyone was seated she plunked her elbows on the table, joined her hands, then leaned forward, resting her chin on her twined fingers. "We're not so tough outside of the group. Which is why we're here. We're so glad you came. We all really appreciate your help."

Cory smirked. "I'm not so sure I've been much help, except for just standing there. But I'm glad it works for you."

Another woman, about their age, also leaned forward toward Cory. "First I was nervous, but I know that with the right guidance, we can learn to defend ourselves properly. Will you come back next time?"

"I hadn't planned on it, but I suppose I could if you need me."

The blond woman glanced at Daphne and then looked back toward Cory. "We're all supposed to take turns bringing a volunteer each week, but not all of us have someone who we can ask. Will you be my volunteer next time, too?"

"Sure. It won't hurt. Much, anyway."

At his comment all the women giggled.

One of the other women spoke up. "I don't have anyone I can bring, either. Would you come as my volunteer, too?"

He stiffened, and Daphne could tell he was forcing a polite smile. "I guess so."

The woman at the end of the table leaned forward. "I don't have anyone, either, and neither does Tiffany. I wonder if Allie might ask if you could help us for the rest of the sessions."

Daphne wasn't sure she wanted Cory to be there every time. While it had helped her for him to be there the first time, the point was that she needed to learn to defend herself against someone she didn't trust, or who would put her in jeopardy. Cory wouldn't do that, and she didn't fear him. When the other ladies brought a man they knew, she wouldn't know him, and that would help motivate her to actually try to cause pain. Except it appeared no one had anyone they could bring.

Fortunately someone changed the subject, but all questions and conversation turned to focus on Cory. When the topic of Cory being a forest ranger came up, while a lot were things she already knew, she did learn a lot more about what he did all year.

She certainly didn't like hearing the story of how a couple of years ago he was recruited to help control a forest fire. She had no idea that forest rangers did so many things, even though it was unrealistic to think that someone had to attend university for so long just to babysit campers for the summer months.

Cory was the first to push his cup away. "It's getting a little late, I need to drive Daphne home, so I think it's time we left."

When Cory stood, so did everyone else. They all walked outside together. They said their goodbyes and as everyone went their separate ways, Cory opened the door to his truck, retrieved the step and put it on the ground, and stood back.

"That was really strange. It's like they were following us, but I guess they all wanted to ask me to be their volunteer."

They'd all been checking him out, Daphne knew, and the more the evening continued, the more they'd all liked what they'd seen.

And, he didn't get it.

Not wanting to point that out, all she did was agree and climb into his truck.

After he backed out of the spot and began to move

forward, he glanced at her quickly and then turned his attention to the road as he pulled into traffic. "Now that we're alone, was there something you wanted to say to me? It looked like you didn't exactly welcome their company, but it would have been rude to decline their invitation to join them."

There was, but the moment was gone now. As well, they only had a few minutes and they would be home, and this was not a conversation she wanted to have with Rick watching through the blinds. "It wasn't important. Are you busy tomorrow? The forecast says it's not going to rain, so it looks like a good day for a walk."

"Sure."

When he pulled up in front of the house, they both looked at the front window at the same time, and both of them saw the movement of the blinds closing.

"Rick knows you're home," he said with a sigh.

Until now, Rick's observance had been a relief. Tonight, though, she suspected that she would be laying awake half the night, wondering why, suddenly, she wanted more than to just say good-night and go separate ways.

She turned to Cory at the same time as he turned to the door and slipped out. He jogged around the truck, opened her door, got the step out from behind her seat, set it on the ground and stepped back.

This time, instead of just grasping the back of the seat for support as she slid out, she extended one hand toward him, forcing him to take it and hold it to help support her as she stuck her foot out to feel for the step before she put her weight on it to get out.

When she had both feet on solid ground, she didn't pull her hand out from his. Her heart quickened when instead of releasing her hand, he gave it a gentle squeeze then reached out so he held both her hands in both of his.

"Good night," he muttered, his voice sounding lower in pitch than his usual tenor.

She looked up at him. The setting was almost romantic. The dark night; being sheltered from the streetlamp by a tall, thick tree. Night crickets chirping.

She wanted to kiss him.

The porch light flashed on, then the glow of light from the front door opening covered them.

Rick stepped out and walked toward them. "Hey, how was your class? Did you take down a creepy guy in three easy steps?"

Cory blinked with the invasion of light. He dropped her hands, stepped back and turned his head toward Rick. "Yeah. The creepy guy was me, and it was four rather painful steps." He turned back to Daphne. "I should go. Do you want me to pick you up after work for our jog in the park, or meet me there?"

Rick's face tightened at Cory's words.

Daphne ignored him. "First I have to come home and change. I'll see you there."

After Cory left, Rick turned to her. "Don't you think you're overdoing it with seeing him every day?"

"I don't see him every day." As the words left her mouth, counting back, maybe not exactly from the chamber of commerce dinner, but not long after that, she did see him almost every day. "Never mind, I take that back. Good night. I'll see you tomorrow."

Before her brother could respond, she turned, entered the house, went into her bedroom and closed the door.

So what if she saw Cory every day. She liked seeing him every day. He also must like seeing her every day, or he wouldn't ask.

She hoped.

"Shh. Don't move."

"I have to." Contrary to his words, Daphne lifted the camera.

Cory gritted his teeth as the Red-Breasted Nuthatch flew away.

This spot was his haven following those days he was trapped behind a desk at head office instead of out in the field. Days that drove him crazy. It probably wasn't very macho, but when he needed to purge the stress from a day of traffic and congestion and then being trapped in a cubicle in a downtown office tower, this was how he did it. Many men went to the gym to hit something to get their frustrations out of their system, but he couldn't do that. Instead he came here to simply sit still.

And now he'd brought his main source of stress to share it with him.

If he lived on the first or second floor, he could

hang a bird feeder on the edge of the balcony of the suite above him and expect visitors all year 'round. On the seventh floor, that didn't happen. So instead, he'd made a bird feeder and hung it in a tree on the small patch of property near the entrance to his apartment building, where he could see it with his binoculars. Many days, even in the rainy winter, he'd just sit on his balcony and watch it, waiting for the birds to enjoy his offerings.

Some days, even though many people probably thought he was crazy, he would take a lawn chair and go sit close to it. As if he didn't see enough birds on a normal work day when he was actually out in the forests or parks. Here, he was taking care of the city birds that didn't have the same feeding opportunities as the country birds.

Often children who lived in his building or nearby buildings would join him.

Today he wasn't wearing his hat. And there were no children. Just him and Daphne.

Even though the Nuthatch had gone, Daphne remained immobile, her camera raised. "I'm going to stay like this until the next one comes. I've never done this before. I think I'm going to put a feeder in my backyard."

"Then you have to make sure you keep something in it, all the time. And after a heavy rain you've got to check the seeds and make sure it's still dry. Moist feed can get bacteria and make the birds sick."

Keeping her camera aimed at the feeder, Daphne turned her head. "Sometimes it's almost hard to get a word out of you, but when you see an animal of any kind, you go into teaching mode. Did you know that?"

He opened his mouth then snapped it shut. "Sorry." More than teaching mode, right now he was in nervous mode, and animals and their habitats was the easiest thing for him to talk about when a silence became awkward.

She smiled. "Don't be sorry. I like that about you. I also like that you make the effort and take the time to do that for the little birdies. You've got the feeder in such a good spot. It's hidden from public view unless you know where to look."

"I'm kind of the only one who can reach it at that height." Wily teens could probably get at it with a ladder, but most of the kids in the neighborhood knew him, at least by sight, so no one touched his feeder.

"This is so calming. Like watching an aquarium."

"I'm not really into fish, but even if I was, they don't allow aquariums in my building."

He watched Daphne, once again totally focused on his bird feeder, taking pictures of every bird that came, including the sparrows.

First she'd come to his place and made it as far as the visitor parking. Now she was in the yard. He hadn't yet invited her up to his apartment because he wasn't sure she would accept. He had to be happy that she would go with him into his truck, which was, as far as he understood, the biggest hurdle she'd had to face. Yet, realistically, it wasn't. A vehicle in a parking lot was still accessible if she became distressed, whereas inside a residence was not.

This time a Pine Siskin came and went; the only movement besides the bird pecking for seed was Daphne's finger, taking about a dozen shots of the same bird. This one was good for photos, as it was relatively rare for a Siskin to be around in the late spring.

As more birds came and went, he saw rather than heard a number of children creeping in and sitting in the grass beside both his and Daphne's chairs. With all the kids around him, here it didn't feel like work. This was his home, and he liked kids. Since he was an only child, when the day came that he was married and it was time to have kids, he wanted lots. Not a baseball team number, but definitely more than two.

He didn't know his father—he'd never even seen a photo of the man whose genes made him. When looking in the mirror he could see some of his mother, in masculine features, but mostly he saw the face of a man he didn't know.

When the day came and he had kids, when they became adults, he wanted them to look in the mirror and like what they saw and be proud of their history, even if it only went back one generation.

His mind wandered. Despite himself, he wondered what kind of kids Daphne would have. Or Daphne and him together.

He knew Daphne had a good relationship with all her family—her brother, her parents and her grandparents on both sides. That was what he wanted for the kids he'd have one day, even though on his side it would only go back to him and his mother. He'd never met his grandparents on his mother's side. He didn't even know if they were alive or, if they were, where they lived. Every time he asked, his mother refused to talk about them. On his father's side, it was even bleaker. The place for his father's name on his birth certificate simply read "Unknown."

He didn't have a heritage behind him but, God willing, he could make one in front of him.

Maybe because the day was unseasonably warm, more and more children came until the grass had become a sea of young bird-watchers, snapping him out of his depressing thoughts.

He was here to relax and share what calmed him, and that's what he was going to do.

Just as Daphne had pointed out, since he now had the usual group of interested bird-watchers around him plus a number of visitors, he began to ask the children who remembered the names of the birds as they came and went. As the children responded, he hoped Daphne liked birds, too. If she didn't, he hoped that she was going to.

As the different common birds arrived, someone in the group correctly named every single one, and he could see Daphne smiling, whether at the children or the birds, he didn't know. The bottom line was that she was smiling, and after that, it didn't matter. It was good.

When a Red Crossbill came, none of the children indicated that they knew it.

"Doesn't anyone know that one's name?" he asked in a stage whisper.

"His name is Charlie!" a little boy called out, causing the bird to fly away and the group to break out into a fit of giggles, which became intermixed with shushes. The group once more became quiet.

"I don't know, Cory," the young boy said. "I never saw one of that kind before."

"It's a Red Crossbill. It's a type of finch, and you don't see them very often in this area. You're very lucky to have seen this one." He hoped Daphne's finger hadn't worn out, and that she hadn't filled up her memory card. This was a rare sighting.

A chorus of "ohh-hhh" cascaded through the sea of children before they again hushed, so the next bird would come.

For about an hour children came and went with the birds, until he stood. "That's it for today. It's getting late, and it's time for the birds to find a place to roost for the night, and so should most of you. Good night."

A few children thanked him, but most of them simply turned and scattered, either running for their parents, who were in groups chatting, or to the main door, where they flooded in.

When Daphne stood, he folded both lawn chairs but then didn't know what to do. Daphne had come in her own car, so he didn't need to drive her home, but if they went anywhere, she would be waiting outside while he took his lawn chairs up to his apartment.

She held up one hand toward him. "Like you said to the kids, it's nearly time for bed, and I've got to get up early in the morning. I need to go in an hour early for a rush project, so it's time for me to go, too. This has been a nice evening. I'll see you tomorrow."

Before he could comment or thank her for coming, she was gone.

At least she'd said the evening was "nice."

Hopefully, *nice* wasn't woman-speak for *boring*.

Chapter 9

"You did what with him?"

Daphne tried not to cringe as her brother glared at her. "I said, we watched birds."

"You're kidding, right?"

"No. That's what we did. He brought out a couple of lawn chairs and a thermos of coffee, and we sat there and watched the birds. He's got a birdfeeder that he hung on the tree outside the door of his apartment block. Then it seemed like all the kids in the neighborhood joined us. It was really different. But it was nice."

Better than nice, it had been great.

Maybe one day she'd even see Charlie the Red Crossbill.

"What else did you do?"

"Nothing. We just sat there and drank coffee and watched the birds. And don't look at me like that."

Rick dragged one hand down his face. "Like what?"

"Like you think I'm crazy. It was actually quite relaxing. We sat there for an hour and a half and watched the birds and he got all the kids to say their names."

Rick shook his head. "Kids? You sat with Cory and a bunch of kids?"

She nodded. "A bunch of kids from the neighborhood joined us and he got them to say the names of the birds. The children got all the names right except one." Which was pretty amazing. Just as Cory claimed, that proved he sat out there often, watching the birds with whoever joined him, and teaching them the species of every bird that came for a snack.

He obviously liked children, which made her wonder why he wasn't married with a minivan full of them. He treated them gently and with kindness.

She'd wondered if he'd been treating her with kid gloves because he knew why she'd been living in a fishbowl, and if it would be different if he hadn't known.

Somehow she didn't think it would be much different. He'd been naturally good with the kids, and she could tell by the glances he'd exchanged with some of the parents that what happened was normal, and happened often.

People trusted him, children liked him, and he liked them back.

He was a good man and she couldn't help but like him. A lot.

She'd met Cory for the first time while she was dating Alex, and now, looking back, she couldn't help but wonder what her life would have been like if she'd met Cory first. She couldn't even imagine Cory being disrespectful of her, much less forcing himself on her. She did know what would happen if they disagreed on something. He did the same thing as his two friends from church did with their wives—the two of them discussed whatever they couldn't agree on and met in the middle.

Yet, as much as she enjoyed her time with him, she needed to understand why he was doing this.

At first she knew he'd taken her to the banquet as a favor to her brother, for which she'd be eternally grateful. She was pretty sure that whatever favor Cory owed had been paid back, and that was probably why Rick couldn't understand why Cory kept seeing her.

All she could do was hope he would continue, because the more she got to know him, the more she liked him. Which, right now, was a lot.

Unless there was something Rick knew that he wasn't telling her.

All she could do was hope it wasn't so.

Cory stood at Daphne's door, wiggled the knot of his tie, and pressed the doorbell.

Instead of Daphne opening it, when it swung inward, Rick stood in the doorframe.

He didn't look happy.

Cory stiffened. "Is she ready? We need to be early today. I have to hand out bulletins." He made a point of glancing over Rick's shoulder, to the living room, where there was no sign of Daphne.

"She's not quite ready yet. This gives us a chance to talk."

Cory couldn't decide if this was good or bad. He remembered back to the night he'd almost kissed Daphne good-night after her first session with the self-defense group. After that night, he didn't know, but he'd felt something change between him and his friend.

It would be good to clear the air.

"Sure." He started to move to enter the house.

Rick stepped forward, blocking his path. "Outside would be better."

This was going to be bad.

Cory purposely lifted his wrist, making it obvious he was checking the time. "I only have a few minutes. She said she'd be ready when I got here."

"I needed her to fix a pocket on my uniform. It won't take her long."

This was going to be really bad.

"Spill. What's up?"

Rick's face tightened. "I don't really like all the time you've been spending with my sister. Things are moving too fast for her, and she's not ready."

Cory didn't know much about women, but something had changed, and it was good. She smiled at him more. She never backed up if he stood too close. A few times when he dropped her off he thought she would respond if he took her in his arms to kiss her good-night, but every time she said she knew Rick was watching, apologized and stepped back.

Often she'd be the first to ask about plans. She texted him at least once a day, sometimes about nothing. Sometimes even if he hadn't been the one to text her first.

Yesterday when he'd told her that he needed to go early to church to hand out bulletins, she asked if he would pick her up instead of going separately and meeting there.

He wanted to take all those things as signs that they were ready to move forward in their relationship. Maybe, just maybe, she was feeling even a fraction of the same way he felt about her.

He met Rick's glare. "You're wrong. She's ready."

Rick crossed his arms over his chest. "That day when you were best man for Brad and Kayla's wedding, I'd given you the job of looking after her at the chamber dinner. That's all it was supposed to be."

"That wasn't the deal. It wasn't limited to just that one day." He cleared his throat and paused, to give his next words more effect. "I'm not doing this just to help her, even though that is important. I'm doing this because I like your sister. A lot. I want what's best for her, and that's to be happy." He didn't say the next words he was thinking. *With me.*

"I know my sister better than you do. I'm not sure that she's ready to be dating."

Cory wondered, really, how Rick would know that. Not long after Brad and Kayla's wedding he'd been with or talked to Daphne every day, meaning she hadn't spent much time with her brother—she'd been with him instead. They'd been to church together every Sunday, as well as his weekly Bible study meetings. He'd been taking her twice a week to the self-defense classes, and been the target male potential assailant every time.

When they had nothing else planned they'd gone for walks, and then short runs. Once they went to the gym where she'd done some rock wall climbing with him. She'd actually been really good at it, probably because she was so small and agile.

They'd also spent a good amount of time at the mall, an activity he didn't really like, but he acquiesced every time because she did.

"I know we're not dating, but we've been spending almost all our time together. I think she *is* ready to start dating." Again, he thought it but didn't say. *With me.*

Rick turned to away, not making eye contact as he spoke. "If she was ready, she'd tell me."

"But she didn't tell you that she still wasn't ready, did she?"

"Not exactly."

Cory checked his watch again. "Tell you what. Why don't you join us for church this morning, and you can see how she interacts with people. I think you'll be surprised." As far as Cory was concerned, Daphne was almost back to her old self, the woman he'd wanted to get to know better, and he had. "Rick, I know how much you care about your sister. I do too."

Before Rick had a chance to reply, Daphne came running down the stairs. "I'm so sorry it took so long. I had a hard time finding the right button, but I did. Let's go."

"Wait. Rick might come with us to church. What do you say, Rick?"

Rick's face tightened. "Sorry, I can't. I have to work this afternoon. I'll talk to you later."

Cory had a feeling he would be indeed be hearing more from Rick, but he no longer cared. He'd said what he needed to say, and as far as he was concerned, he'd made his intentions clear. Whatever happened, happened. He was going to go for what he wanted, and that was earning the key to Daphne's heart.

He pulled his keys out of his pocket. "Let's go. If we hurry we can still be there in good time before the congregation starts to arrive. We'll be the best bulletin team that church has ever seen."

"How many teams are there, exactly?"

He felt his cheeks turning warm. "We might be the only one."

"Then I'm up for the challenge." She turned to Rick. "It's too bad you have to work. We always go out for lunch after the service with some friends. Maybe next time?"

Rick frowned. "Sure. Another time."

Somehow Cory doubted it, but it was probably always a possibility.

Chapter 10

Daphne couldn't help but grin ear to ear as Allie handed her the certificate. The room full of women, and Cory, applauded.

"Congratulations to all of you," Allie said as she raised one hand to encompass the whole group. "Everyone here has passed the Level One session. Let's all give ourselves and each other a big round of applause!"

After the applause died down, Allie moved to highlight Cory, standing next to Daphne. "Now let's give a big round of applause to our number-one volunteer, Cory!"

The applause for Cory was more enthusiastic than the applause for all the ladies completing the sessions. He wasn't only the number-one volunteer, he was the only volunteer. At the recognition, Cory's ears turned red.

As the commotion died, Allie clapped her hands to get everyone's attention. "I've got coffee and snacks on the table in the back. Everyone enjoy!"

Everyone made their way to the back of the room, including Cory.

Daphne could tell Cory was trying to get away from the crowd of women, but as he approached the tray of doughnuts they surrounded him. Daphne almost smiled, watching him trying to decide which doughnut to pick.

Then Susie placed her hand on Cory's arm.

Cory froze, his fingers inches away from his favorite doughnut, the one with the chocolate icing and colored sprinkles.

Susie smiled up at him. Daphne had noticed that today, Susie had on a face full of makeup and sexy red lipstick. Her hair was artfully arranged to look just out of place enough that a man would want to smooth it into place.

"Hi, Cory." Susie practically purred. "After this is over, how would you like to join me for a drink? Or maybe, if you don't want to do that, we could go catch a movie sometime?"

"Uh…I…"

Daphne felt her teeth clench. She was more than aware that a number of the ladies were attracted to Cory. She'd thought she'd been obvious in showing that he wasn't available. They'd always arrived

together, and left together. Meaning, they were together.

Almost like a flashback, her own words echoed
in her head. When she'd first introduced Cory to the
group, she'd introduced him only as her brother's
friend.

Maybe at the time he was, but that was then. She'd
come to know him differently now, and he was so
much more. She'd never known anyone like him, and
probably never would again. She didn't want to lose
him, or allow what had developed between them to
change or be compromised.

She had to do something and she had to do it now.

Before Cory could say something coherent,
Daphne stepped closer, standing right beside them.
She stared down at Susie's hand, still attached to
Cory's arm. Flashing Susie a smile that was overly
sweet, she glared down at Susie's fingers, then looked
up to give Susie her best glare of death.

"Sorry, but Cory and I have plans."

The second Susie made eye contact, she yanked
her hand away then shuffled backward. "Oh," she
muttered and then turned around and walked away.

Cory's eyes widened. "Did she just ask me out?"

Instead of looking up at Cory, Daphne looked
around them. Most of the other ladies were watching them. She turned to him. "I think so. I hope you
weren't going to accept."

He shook his head. "No."

She lowered her voice. "Don't look now, but most
of them are watching you."

"Really? Why? All I'm doing is getting a dough-nut."

Daphne almost wanted to smack some sense into him. Every week, all the ladies had been keeping a close eye on Cory, and an even closer eye on the inter-action between the two of them. She hadn't intended to do anything about it, but now that one of them had tried to make a move on him, she found herself feel-ing possessive of him.

"Because a few of them are probably hoping you are going to ask them out."

"Out where? We don't need to go out for coffee and doughnuts tonight. Allie has everything here."

She looked up at him. "You don't get it, do you? They're trying to see if we're really together or not, and if not, a few of them have hopes that you'll ask them out on a date."

"Oh." As a silence hung between them; she could almost see the gears working in his head. "They seem to be nice ladies and all that, but I'm really not inter-ested. I don't want to hurt anyone's feelings. What should I do?"

A million pictures zoomed through her head, es-pecially one.

"I know. Come with me."

Before he could question her, she twined her fin-gers with his and gave him a gentle tug. He picked up on her hint and started walking with her toward the hall leading to the washrooms.

"Where are we going?"

"Away from the crowd for a few minutes. If we

hide around the corner they'll make a bunch of assumptions on what we're doing, and then they'll leave you alone."

While looking up, she felt the brush of Cory's fingers on her shoulder. "If I get what you're telling me, the assumption they'll be making is that some hanky-panky is going on between us. If that was going to happen, we'd be standing closer together."

As in a dream, Cory moved closer to her. Slowly, he extended one hand and brushed his fingers lightly against her cheek. His head tipped to one side. Standing so close, the height difference between them hit her as never before.

If they were kissing, to make the right contact, either he would be shorter or she would be taller, or both. Right now, for something to happen, the logistics weren't right. He towered over her by more than a foot. A romantic embrace with a kiss, as done in the movies, wasn't physically possible. The top of her head didn't even reach his armpit.

Words failed her.

He raised one finger in the air. "I have an idea." He dropped down so one knee touched the ground, and with his other foot flat on the ground, his other knee remained bent in front of him. "Sit on my knee. Let's see what happens."

"I don't know," she muttered, but did as he said anyway, trying to balance herself on his knee. It didn't feel secure, until his hands surrounded her waist.

He sure had big hands.

First she looked down at his hands, then up at his face. Right into his eyes. Almost level.

"This would work," she whispered, almost in shock to be so close, in a dimly lit hallway.

"I think so, too."

At his words, her eyes fluttered shut. The warmth of his lips brushed hers, making her head spin and her heart pound. Without thinking, she raised her hands and cupped his cheeks, finding them rough with the day's growth of his beard.

At her touch, he tilted his head slightly and the brush became a real kiss. Slow, warm...and the most romantic thing that had ever happened to her.

Behind her, someone gasped.

They separated and Daphne scrambled to her feet as though someone had dumped a pail of cold water over her head.

Cory's eyes popped open and he pushed himself back up to a standing position.

Daphne spun around to see Susie standing in the hallway. Susie stiffened and strode into the ladies' washroom, slamming the door behind her.

She wasn't sure what had just happened, but something had. She wasn't sure if she had kissed him, or if he had kissed her, but a kiss had definitely happened.

Behind her, Cory cleared his throat. "I think we should get back to the party."

She didn't know if she could face the crowd. Too much was running through her head right now.

In the back of her mind, something told her that she should have been afraid, but she wasn't.

She should have wanted to run away, to escape, but she didn't. She wanted to go to Cory, to wrap her arms around him and hold him tight, and to have him do the same to her.

The words of her counselor echoed through her head. When the time was right for her to move on and put what Alex had done behind her, she would know. It would just happen.

Something had happened, but she wasn't sure what.

But before she did anything rash, there was someone she needed to talk to.

She needed to go home and pray about this.

Daphne shuffled backward and cleared her throat. "I think I need to go home."

For the first time, today Cory had been tied up with some paperwork when it had been time to get ready for the session. To let him finish his work, instead of him going to her place to pick her up, they'd come in separate cars. He didn't need to drive her home.

She cleared her throat. "I don't think you need to follow me home today. It's not that late. I'll be fine."

He rammed his hands into his pockets. "I don't like it, but if that's what you want, I'll respect it. Will I see you tomorrow?"

Tomorrow was Saturday, and she could and probably would spend the whole day with him.

If she was going to follow this through, she had to do the bravest thing possible. "Yes. Tomorrow Rick is having some friends over. Instead of coming over to my house, how about if I pick up something for lunch, and go to your place? So we can talk. Would noon work?"

His brows raised and his eyes widened. "Sure. That would be good."

That was what Daphne was hoping for—that it would indeed be good. She cleared her throat. "Then I'll see you tomorrow."

Right on time, at noon the buzzer for the front door sounded.

The time from when he hit the button to open the main entrance to the time he heard her knock on his apartment door was the longest two minutes and twenty-seven seconds of his life.

When he opened the door, she smiled up at him.

She was the most beautiful thing he'd ever seen. Since Brad and Kayla's wedding, she'd put on about ten to fifteen pounds, and with all the exercise they'd done, it was all muscle—and in all the right places. She looked great. Really great.

She held up a bag. "I brought lunch. Are you hungry?" She giggled. "Silly question. Of course you're hungry. Where's the kitchen?"

He jerked one thumb over his shoulder, pointing down the hall. "That way."

Without hesitation, she walked past him and straight to the kitchen, where the coffeepot was just finishing the last drips.

"Great timing. I'm dying for a coffee right now. I never drink coffee when I'm driving. Even though it's not as distracting as talking on the cell phone, I don't do it. I don't talk on the phone, either." Her voice lowered. "My brother's a cop, you know." She grinned at him, then lowered her head to the bag.

It was a good thing she wasn't looking at him. He couldn't grin back.

While she pulled everything out of the bag, Cory poured two cups of coffee, put in the right amount of cream and sugar, and set the mugs on the table.

After a quick prayer, they dug into the food.

"Nice place you've got."

"Thanks." He'd been cleaning for hours. He'd started last night, and the place had never been so tidy.

"You probably have a good view from up here."

"It's okay." He'd picked this side of the building, even though the rent was a bit more, because he loved the view.

"Does that big truck of yours fit in the underground parking here, or do you have a spot outside?"

"Outside." Not trusting the height restriction on the sign posted at the entrance to the underground parking, he'd used a tape measure, just to be sure. Even if he'd taken the antenna off, his truck still wouldn't have fit.

For every question she asked him, all he could come up with was one- or two-word answers. He was so lame, but his brain just wouldn't work.

When they finished eating, she stuffed the wrappers into the bag, then walked to the kitchen sink and opened the cupboard door to stuff it into the garbage, with no question as to where it would be.

"Let's go into the living room. I want to see the view." Without waiting for him, she refilled her coffee mug then walked straight to the patio door. Instead of stopping, she opened the door and walked out onto the balcony. "Wow. This is spectacular. Are you coming?"

Without speaking, he joined her on the balcony.

She sank down into one of the chairs, turning her head toward the city skyline, so he did the same.

With a big sigh, she sipped her coffee. "I thought I was going to be nervous coming here, but I'm not." She turned to him. "I'm good. Really. I was going to say that you look more nervous than I do, but I don't think I look nervous, because I'm not. I feel good. Like this is really right. It's okay. Relax."

The weight of a downed cedar lifted off his shoulders. "That's good to hear. I really don't know what to say."

"Then let's just talk."

He doubted she wanted to hear about the last Seahawks game. "About what?"

She set her coffee cup on the table, folded her hands in front of her and leaned forward. "Us. Let's talk about us."

It was almost as if Cory's life flashed before his eyes. The past few months had seemed like forever, yet today was moving at light speed.

He gulped. This was it. The moment he'd been both dreaming about and dreading. "Us?"

She looked down at her hands, which made him even more nervous. "I was thinking about it last night and… I hope this isn't being too forward, but I really like you." Her face turned a bit pink, and he hoped it was because she was thinking about the same thing that flashed through his mind—the short kiss they'd shared before they were so rudely interrupted. "I hope you feel the same way, so I want to ask you where you want to go with our relationship." She looked up at him. "We do have a relationship, don't we?"

Relationship. That was what he wanted more than anything else in the world. A permanent relationship with Daphne. One where they could be together most of the time, all the time. They would see each other at their best, and their worst, and still want to be together anyway. To share their joys and sorrows, and face the world together. He wanted the whole thing. The wedding, the mortgage, the kids, the dog and maybe a cat. A real relationship.

He cleared his throat. "Yeah. We do."

"That's great." She smiled at him. A real smile. From her heart. Like the kind of smile the woman in a movie did before the big kiss that ended the movie with the happily-ever-after ending scene that women loved so much and made men groan.

This was it. It hadn't happened the conventional way he thought a permanent relationship usually started, but it was there. If he wanted it. And he did.

This was the time he should have jumped up and grabbed her and kissed her, and she would kiss him back, this time without someone interrupting.

But he couldn't.

He folded his hands on the table in front of him and stiffened his back. "Before we go any further, there's something about me you need to know."

Chapter 11

Daphne gulped. The good lunch she'd just eaten turned to a rock in her stomach. In the movies, this was the lead-in for the speaker to say he or she had a life-threatening disease, and the other would pledge their unending love and support. Then, somehow, by the end of the movie, after a lot of hard work and sacrifice, together they would overcome the battle. The closing of the movie promised they would live happily ever after, and life went on.

But this wasn't a movie. This was real life. Maybe this was something that couldn't be fixed. But even if it couldn't, whatever he said, she hoped it was something they could battle together. "Go ahead."

"I've never told you about how I became a forest ranger." He paused, letting the silence hang.

"I thought people became rangers because they loved nature and the great outdoors."

He turned away, not making eye contact, which she didn't think was a good sign.

"While I do like getting away into the wilderness, that wasn't what started me being a ranger."

"Then how did you decide to be a forest ranger?" She couldn't see it being the kind of job a person fell into. She also couldn't see why the reason he became a forest ranger was so important right now.

"I got into it through community service."

"Community service?" A million pictures swam through her head. Community service was usually done as a means to reduce a sentence or to avoid jail time after being found guilty of a crime. "I don't understand."

He finally looked at her, the eye contact so intense it almost burned. She wanted to look away, but couldn't. "Just before I became legal age, I was arrested for assault and battery. The assault and battery charges were dropped, but I did get charged with a misdemeanor for property damage. Instead of going to juvvie, I did community service, which ended up being planting trees. While I was doing the tree planting thing, I grew up and became an adult. That led to the ranger in charge taking me aside and prompting me to become a forest ranger."

All she could do was stare at him. "Assault and battery? Property damage?" She shuffled backward, as far as the chair would allow. The picture of Cory beating a man to a pulp while smashing things around him swam through her head almost like a movie in slow motion. Considering his size and strength, he could probably kill someone with his bare hands. But he didn't say murder or manslaughter. It was just assault and battery. *Just*.

"Who did you assault?" She gulped. "How bad was he hurt?" She gulped again. "And why?"

He continued to speak with his head still lowered, staring intently at his hands. "I broke a few bones, but he made a full recovery. It could have been worse. In the thick of it, I had him up off the ground, ready to give him a good one to the face. In the right place, a hit like that would have broken his neck. But something stopped me, almost like God telling me that was enough, to stop. Instead of that last punch I threw him into the wall and walked away." He raised his head, but didn't look at her. He turned toward the horizon, his eyes unfocused. "I walked around the block a few times to clear my head. That was when I asked God to come into my life, the actual moment I became a Christian. When I got home the police and an ambulance were there, and I was arrested."

Daphne couldn't speak. All she could do was watch Cory as he stared blankly into the skyline.

"You asked who he was and why I did it. In front of me, my mother called him her boyfriend, but he wasn't. Hank was her drug dealer. I'd just found out we'd been evicted for not paying the rent. She'd spent the rent money, which I'd earned at my part-time job, specifically for the rent, on drugs. How it started was that I had just got home, and as I walked inside I heard

Hank telling my mother that if she smuggled some cocaine into the country he'd give her the fix she needed and enough money to pay the rent."

Daphne's mind swam as she tried to process the details. "Is that when you hit him?"

"No. I was pretty mad, but I did try to reason with him. At first Hank told me to butt out, but I wouldn't. I told him to leave my mother alone and to get out of our place and never come back. At that point the situation deteriorated pretty fast. I never saw it coming. He swung out and hit me, and everything went downhill. When he woke up in the hospital the next day he said he wasn't going to press charges, and I was released. He should have pressed charges, but I'm sure you can understand why a drug dealer with a record wouldn't want to be in the court system, even as a plaintiff instead of a defendant."

She couldn't imagine Cory in such a fight, but it obviously had happened. "I guess your mother called the police while the fight was going on because she couldn't stop it?"

He shrugged his shoulders. "Actually, she didn't. After all, I was fighting with a known drug dealer. Her drug dealer. The last thing she wanted was the police coming in at that moment. When the fight was over and I left, I found out later that she'd flushed the drugs he'd had on him down the toilet, and then called the ambulance. I'm guessing the police came later when the medics discovered who the victim was. You know, when you read in the paper about an incident when someone is 'known to the police'? Well, he was really known to the police, so the ambulance guys called the police. But with no drugs found in the house, the only one who got arrested that day was me."

"I can't believe your mother would let the police take you away."

"She couldn't have stopped them, but she didn't even try. It was obviously me who did it. They hauled me away, but since I was a juvenile and he said that he wasn't going to press charges the police took me home after a night in detention."

"Your mother must have been glad to have you back."

He shook his head. "Not really. Remember she'd flushed the drugs he'd brought down the toilet, and with her dealer in the hospital, my mother was pretty mad. Also, we'd just been evicted. When the police dropped me off the landlord was there, because of the damage. Also there'd been a lot of buzz in the neighborhood about what happened. While they were arguing I ran inside to change, then I went to my part-time job. Word that I'd been arrested for beating up one of the local dealers had gotten around really fast. I didn't even make it to my station. I got fired because they didn't want a person like me working there, even though all I was doing was slinging burgers."

"Can they do that?"

"They can do whatever they want. If I wanted the job back I would have had to take them to court, and I wasn't in a position to do that. When I got home, after fighting with the landlord, my mother kicked me out, and my landlord charged me with property damage. Those charges did stick because I was so close to being legal age when it happened. By the time it hit the courts, I was legal age, so they couldn't send me to a juvenile detention center. Fortunately, property damage is only a misdemeanor—hence the community service. That was why planting trees up at the camp worked really well. It was hard work but I had three squares and a roof over my head."

All Daphne could do was stare at him. "What did you do in the meantime? You said your mother had kicked you out,"

"She did. Until the court case came up I had to sleep on the couch of whoever would take me in that day and pretty much beg for them to feed me, because no one would hire me after I got fired."

She couldn't imagine begging people to house and feed him. It also meant he had been living out of a suitcase, and even though he didn't say it, she wondered if he spent any time living on the streets with the vagrants.

"What did you do when the tree planting was finished?"

He sighed. "The ranger in charge felt bad for me because I didn't have a job and I didn't have a place to live. When the tree planting gig was over he set me up with a part-time job with the parks board and a friend of his took me in for cheap room and board while I finished high school however I could. I managed to get my GED. He later co-signed so I could get a loan for college to be a forest ranger. When I graduated he gave me a good reference and pulled some strings and I got the job. The rest is history."

"Your boss cosigned your college loan?"

"Yup. And he's still my boss, so I can't default on the loan."

While it was good that he had a stable relationship with his supervisor, she couldn't rid her mind of the reality that Cory had beaten someone so badly that it required hospitalization. Even if it was a drug dealer, the man was still a person.

"Does your mother still see that man…Hank?"

"Yes. He's still her drug dealer. The only good thing is that when she spent a few days with nothing in her system she saw what it was doing to her. She's not a hard-core addict, but she's definitely hooked. She gives it up for a while, but she always goes back. She lives in a run-down boarding house and spends all her spare money on drugs. At least she's able to maintain a job and she's got a car now."

Daphne remembered Cory getting a gas card for his mother for Mother's Day. It now made so much sense. In a very sad kind of way.

He turned to face her. "When she's talking to me, I try to get her to go into rehab and to come to church with me, but she refuses. She says God can't help her, but I know He can. She knows she needs help, but she won't take it. I've found a place that can help her that my pastor recommended, but she won't go."

Daphne tried to picture it, but she had no experience with that kind of life. All she knew was what she read. But she did know that most of what children learned when they were young was by example. If his mother was a habitual drug user from his childhood days, his daily exposure to it would teach him that drug use was normal, because that's what he saw every day.

"Have you ever used drugs?" She held her breath, waiting for his answer.

"Not really. Probably less than what the average kid would try. I was always focused on sports, always on the school teams. They had policies about not using drugs, and I was one of the few who listened."

She probably should have been picturing him being the star of the basketball team, but like a bystander who couldn't pull themself away from a train wreck, the mental picture of Cory pummeling another man played over and over in her head.

Regardless of the reason, Cory had lost his temper and caused serious injury. This was more than just a fistfight; he had sent a man to the hospital—with his bare hands. "You'd mentioned property damage. What kind of property damage?" Even though she had a feeling she wouldn't like the answer, like the train-wreck syndrome, she had to know.

"When I threw him into the wall he didn't just dent the wall, he made a hole. My mother didn't have any money to fix it, and it was more than the damage deposit. The landlord took us to court over it, both of us. Even though I was a juvenile, they still charged me. That's why I had to perform the community service. I did that instead of having to pay for the repairs. That's why my mother had a hard time finding another place."

Daphne couldn't imagine the force it would take to throw a person so hard it made a hole in the wall. All she could do was stare at him. In her mind's eye scenes from the *Incredible Hulk* played out—a being so strong he could do anything, except control his temper when he became angry.

"I know how bad that sounds, and it is bad. But it really was self-defense. I would never use my size and strength against anyone. I want to defend the defenseless, not hurt them."

Daphne stared at him; begging her with his eyes like a beaten puppy dog. But he wasn't helpless—far from it. People were helpless against him.

Regardless of the fact that he said he'd only been defending himself, the results had been catastrophic. Ever since she'd known him, even though they'd had disagreements, she'd never seen him in a situation that tried his patience or his temper. If that was how he defended himself, the easygoing Cory she knew, or at least thought she knew, was a different person when things didn't go his way.

"Why are you telling me this now?"

"Because I don't want you to find out later from someone else." He cleared his throat and his voice dropped to barely above a whisper. "Because I want you to understand…" He paused, making direct eye contact. "Because I've fallen in love with you."

A silence thicker than the dead of a moonless night hung in the air between them. Cory could even hear himself breathing. Ever since he'd met Daphne at the mall that first time they'd had dinner together, he'd known the history hanging over his head was something he had to tell her. The more they'd gotten to know each other, the more pressing it became—he'd wanted the day he told her he loved her to be full of romance and hope for the future.

Instead he felt the possibilities of his future with Daphne crumbling into bits and being blown away by the winds.

He wasn't a fighter. He'd only been in one fight in his life, and he'd just told her about it.

Most women he'd met would have excused it as an error of teenage angst. At the time his life had fallen apart, but with God's help he'd been able to rise above it and do good—for animals, people and nature. But Daphne wasn't most women. She needed a man who could protect her and never lift a finger to hurt her or threaten her, or anyone else, in any way. He was that man, except for that one day. Because of the magnitude of that one day, he'd had to tell her about it. To hide the truth would have been a lie, and he couldn't do that.

"It's in the past, but it *is* my past."

At his words, she froze and looked at him like a deer caught in the headlights of an oncoming truck.

"Does my brother know this?"

"No. It's not something I walk around telling people. I was a juvenile, so my records are sealed. But it did make the news at the time, so what happened is public record. In the end, what's on record is a misdemeanor, no time served, only community service."

"You beat someone so badly he was taken away in an ambulance. Why didn't you tell me sooner?"

"It's not something I'm proud of. I was waiting for the right moment, and it didn't happen."

His heart sank, waiting for her to say something, anything, but nothing came.

He couldn't blame her for being afraid of him.

He steeled his strength—saying it out loud was harder than anything he'd done in life. "This changes things, doesn't it?"

"Yes. It does. I'm sorry. I need time to think."

He felt himself go cold from head to toe. "I understand."

"I need to go."

He didn't try to stop her. He just watched as she dashed into the living room, grabbed her purse and ran out the door.

Not knowing why, he stayed on the balcony and waited, watching the pathway leading to the building's main door. After a few minutes Daphne appeared. She ran out the main entrance and straight for her car. It took off so fast he wondered if the tires had squealed.

Over the past few months he'd done his best to help her regain her confidence and not be afraid of every dark corner. She'd built up her strength and stamina, and most of all, courage and street smarts. Now she no longer needed her brother at her side every time she went someplace other than work.

At the same time, she no longer needed him, either. She'd earned herself the promotion at work, and she was well on the way to get on with her life.

Without him.

He didn't know what he was going to do without her. He'd known for a long time that he wasn't what she saw as her Mr. Right—he was not a skinny accountant. Even though he wasn't what she thought she wanted, he had to prove he was what she needed.

If only he could figure out how.

Chapter 12

Daphne pulled the car to the side of the road, stopped and looked out the window at the entrance to the highway.

She couldn't go home.

If she went home she would talk to Rick. She didn't know much about sealed juvenile records, but she did know herself well enough to know that if she saw Rick right now, she would tell him what she knew about Cory. Regardless of how she felt, what he'd said was in confidence, and not up to her to repeat—especially to one of his friends. Once said, words could not be unsaid. Even if she never saw Cory again, she couldn't destroy his friendship with her brother.

But was that what she wanted, to never see him again?

She really didn't know.

All she knew was the more she thought about it, while there was a lot he had told her, there was a lot he hadn't.

She couldn't see the Cory she knew losing his temper that way. She just couldn't. Yes, his mother had spent the money he'd worked so hard to earn on drugs instead of the rent. Still, knowing Cory's gentle nature, she couldn't see him losing his temper to that degree. She felt as though he'd given her only the bare facts, but not all the details.

She had to find out what he hadn't said.

That day, three people were there. She'd already talked to him. She obviously wasn't going to find the drug dealer and talk to him. The only person left was his mother. Even though the relationship was strained, Cory's mother was the only person who could give her the answers she needed.

Daphne didn't know the exact address, but she remembered the name of the street from seeing the Mother's Day card before Cory had mailed it, and she also remembered that his mother's name was Kathy.

If his mother had a landline and not a cell phone, she would hopefully be searchable online.

Daphne pulled her cell phone out of her purse, set it to check the web, and sure enough, came up with an address on the street he'd written on the envelope. She entered it into her GPS and was soon on her way.

Just as Cory had said, it was a run-down neighborhood. The boarding house her GPS led her to was no different than any other house on the block—in poor repair. Daphne told herself that she knew enough self-defense moves that she would be safe here in the middle of the day.

After making double sure she'd locked her doors, she made her way to the door.

Holding her breath, she knocked and waited.

A taller-than-average woman who had the same almost-black hair as Cory and a feminine version of the same chin answered.

"Are you Kathy, Cory's mother?"

The woman's face paled. "Who are you? Has something happened to him?"

Daphne shook her head. "No. He's fine. I'm a friend of his, and I wonder if I can talk to you about something."

The color came back into Kathy's face and at the same time her eyes narrowed and her lips tightened. "What? Has he done something?"

Daphne didn't think this was a good sign, but she wasn't going to leave. "I know things are a bit strained between you and your son, but I wanted to ask you a few questions about him."

Kathy's eyes narrowed even more. "Are you pregnant?"

The question should have startled her, but it didn't. She'd known for a long time that Cory was the son of a single mother and had never known his father. She wondered if this was the same reaction Kathy had gotten from her own parents, who had disowned her.

She shook her head. "No. Nothing like that. I just

want to talk. Could we find somewhere private? Can I take you out for coffee and a doughnut?" As the words came out of her mouth, she remembered Cory saying his mother wasn't good with money.

Daphne made a point of checking her watch. "I just realized the time. I know it's early, so if you haven't had dinner, I could take you out where we could grab a burger."

Kathy stiffened and crossed her arms over her chest. "What do you want?"

Daphne shook her head. "Nothing. I just want to ask a you a few questions about him as a teen. What he was like."

Kathy remained silent for a few seconds, then nodded. "I'll go get my purse."

When the door closed in her face, Daphne wondered if that was a hint to go away and not come back, but the door did open again. Kathy came out carrying a worn handbag and, unless Daphne was mistaken, she had run a brush through her shaggy hair.

In her car, she remembered passing a fast-food restaurant on the way there, so that's where she headed.

"What's your relationship with Cory? You obviously know him well enough to have found me."

Daphne sucked in a deep breath and tried to appear relaxed. "We're friends. But he told me something from his younger days today, and I need to know more."

Beside her, Kathy gasped. "He told you, didn't he?"

"About what happened with him and Hank? Yes. He did."

A silence hung between them. When she stopped at the red light, Daphne turned to Kathy. "If you want, I can take you home."

"You want to ask me what happened that day, don't you?"

"Yes."

Again, the silence hung.

Kathy sighed and turned her head to look out the window, presumably so Daphne couldn't see her face.

"I've lived that day over and over. Everyone made a lot of mistakes that day. Sure. Ask me anything you want."

She didn't say anything more until they were at the restaurant and had their meals in front of them. While they ate Daphne tried her best to make small talk, even though she was the only one talking. Kathy simply ate and nodded every once in a while at something she said.

When they both had finished eating and only had their drinks to finish, Daphne felt the time was as right as it would ever be. "I'm just going to come right out and say it. I hope you'll answer just as openly as I'm going to ask. What happened that day? Cory told me what he heard and his side of the story of the fight with Hank. Now I'd like to hear yours."

Kathy lowered her half-finished drink to the table. "That was a really low point in my life, and I wasn't thinking very rationally. I was starting to get the shakes, and I don't remember everything that happened, but I'll never forget when Cory walked in…"

Kathy sighed, then continued. "If Cory told you that Hank started the fight, he was telling the truth. He also didn't lie when he said that Hank spat on him then threw his beer at Cory's face. I don't think Cory could see when Hank started hitting him. I was so shocked I didn't know what to do. I was so strung out that all I could think about was that I hoped the cops didn't come, because I didn't want to get arrested."

"Cory told me that." But now she knew he hadn't told her the whole story.

"I don't know how, but Cory managed to focus just as Hank aimed the empty bottle at his face. I remember screaming, thinking that if Hank hit my son in the face with a beer bottle it could knock him out and kill him. Then suddenly Cory grabbed Hank's hand and ducked. The bottle flew out of Hank's hand, bounced off Cory's face, fell to the floor and smashed. Hank moved to kick Cory, yelling that he was going to pay for that… I remember wondering why Hank would say that, because at that time Cory hadn't done anything but grab his hand. Then Hank yelled at me that if I tried to gang up on him, I'd be sorry. I was already sorry, but I didn't want to make it worse. Then he started yelling that I was going to pay, too. He said he'd kill Cory. And me, too."

She paused as Daphne watched, speechless.

"I saw a flash—I think it was a knife—then he kicked Cory. But instead of Cory falling, he suddenly went crazy. He moved so fast—he'd always been good at sports, you know.

"He broke Hank's arm and cracked a couple of ribs. I thought he was going to punch Hank in the nose when he threw Hank against the wall so hard that the wall busted. Then Cory turned around and walked out."

This was definitely a different version than what Cory had told her. If he hadn't been able to disable Hank, it sounded as though Hank wouldn't have stopped until he'd seriously disabled Cory or even killed him.

Cory had given her a very tamed-down version of what had really happened. She could only guess that it was so she wouldn't hate his mother. And that said a lot about him.

"What you've told me really helps a lot." Knowing what Cory had been up against, she knew she would never have to fear him. Considering the way he'd been attacked, he could have done so much worse. Not only had he defended himself against a crazed drug dealer, he'd also defended his mother—a mother who had not treated him very well.

Kathy's eyes welled up and she wiped her sleeve across her face. "I know I should have done something, but I didn't. All I could think about was that if I didn't stand up for Hank, he'd cut me off. I'm a terrible mother. I knew right then that Cory would be better off without me. I know it was wrong, but I was still strung out at the time. I kicked him out and told him not to come back. Now he's got a good life for himself, and I want to keep it that way."

All Daphne could do was feel sorry for Cory's mother. In a skewed way, Kathy's actions had forced Cory to make a better life for himself, but being the man he was, he would have done it anyway.

Daphne started to reach out to cover Kathy's hand with hers, but pulled back at the last second. Kathy didn't seem as if she wanted to be touched by a stranger. "I really don't know what it's like for you, and I didn't come to try to talk you into going to rehab. But Cory's right. It will help you. I don't know what it's like to be addicted to anything, but I know it is possible that, with some help, you can pull yourself out of it."

Kathy sniffled, then blew her nose in her napkin. "I can't afford rehab. I can barely afford to live."

"Cory told me he'd pay for it."

She shook her head and blew her nose again. "I can't let him do that."

This time, Daphne did reach out to lay her fingers on top of Kathy's hand. "But he told me he wants to."

"Okay. Last time I talked to him he said he had a place in mind for me."

Daphne opened her mouth to tell Kathy that she'd been going to group therapy sessions and they really helped, but stopped herself. "Okay? Really?"

Kathy's lower lip quivered. "Really."

Daphne didn't know what to do, but she had a feeling that whatever it was, it needed to be done right away, before Kathy changed her mind. "I don't have any of the information. Can I call Cory?"

"Okay. I'm tired of living like this. There's got to be something better."

"There is. Let me call Cory." Daphne reached for her cell phone, in the outside pocket of her purse, right next to pocket containing the can of bear spray.

It only took her a few seconds to hit the button to speed-dial Cory. He answered quickly.

"It's me. Daphne. Don't ask questions. I'm with your mother, and she's said she wants to try rehab. I need you to find all the information she says you've got and come here."

"Where are you? Are you at her place?"

"No. We're at…" Daphne looked up at the menu board and read the name of the restaurant. "It's about five minutes from her place. Do you know where that is?" For a second she thought of taking Kathy back home to wait for Cory, but she didn't want to do anything that would allow her to perhaps become more comfortable and change her mind. "We're going to stay here and wait for you."

"I'll be there as fast as I can."

She didn't think this was a good time to tell him not to speed or to say out loud that her brother was a cop. "Okay. See you soon."

After he disconnected the call, she tucked her phone back into its pocket, turned to Kathy and tried to give her a friendly smile. "Until he gets here, how would you like to tell me what Cory was like as a little boy. Was he always good at sports?"

* * *

The whole way to the restaurant, Cory watched the speedometer, sticking precisely to the posted limits. He wanted to speed, but Daphne's unspoken words that her brother was a cop, that she often repeated, kept echoing through his head.

He didn't know how or why she'd met his mother. He didn't know what his mother had said to Daphne about that night. She'd told him that she didn't remember a thing except that he'd attacked Hank, totally unprovoked.

It hadn't been unprovoked. Hank had tried to kill him, and Hank had said that when Cory was dead, Hank was going to kill his mother, too.

Daphne didn't need to hear that. He'd pulled himself completely away from that kind of lifestyle. He'd never participated in it in the first place, only watched from a distance. He now regretted giving her the scaled-down version of the events of that day, because that was surely why she'd gone to his mother, to find out more.

Except now she'd met his mother and that wasn't a pretty sight if his mother was again strung out on drugs.

For years he'd hoped and prayed for the day his mother would consent and go to rehab. He didn't know why now, or what part Daphne had played, but whatever the reason, he would thank God in his prayers tonight.

He would also hope and pray that it didn't turn Daphne off so much she would refuse to see him again because of his less-than-stellar upbringing. And that maybe, Daphne could even envision his mother in her future.

Finally he pulled into the parking lot. Seeing Daphne's car made his heart pound. Not only had Daphne called him, but his mother had made that important initial decision.

He couldn't blow it now—on both counts.

When he walked in he spotted them immediately. He couldn't see Daphne's face, but he could see his mother's. Her eyes were red, as though she'd been crying.

It didn't look good.

The second his mother saw him her eyes widened, she slapped her hands over her mouth, made a choking sound, and started crying again.

This really didn't look good.

He quickened his pace, hurrying without running, so as not to cause a scene.

"Mom. Daphne," he muttered as he slid into the empty seat beside Daphne. "Here I am. I brought all my stuff."

His mother nodded without speaking as more tears poured out of her eyes.

Daphne rested one hand on top of his, halting the question of asking how they'd met.

Daphne wrapped her fingers over top of his hand and gave it a squeeze. "Your mom and I have had a good talk. Do you have that phone number?"

He reached into his back pocket and pulled the card out of his wallet, where it had been for years, waiting for the time when she would ask for it. "Yeah. Except it's Saturday. I hope they pick up and it doesn't go to voice mail."

"It shouldn't. I'm sure they have someone answering on the weekends."

If not, he could call his pastor as the next best option.

When a real person answered, a burn started at the backs of his eyes. This really was it. He identified himself and gave them the file number so he wouldn't have to repeat all the personal details, something he was glad for in this public place.

When they were ready, they asked him to hand the phone to his mother, so he did.

His mother listened and nodded a few times. "Yes. I can do that. I think that's a good idea. But I need to ask my son."

She covered the mouthpiece of the phone with one hand and turned to him. "I might not need to take much time off work. They said they have some programs that are only two days a week. I think I really can do this. He says he can see me now, to talk to me and ask more questions. Will you come with me?"

"Of course I will." Cory's heart pounded in his chest. It was really happening. However it got to this point, he owed it to Daphne.

His mother ended the conversation and looked up at him, her eyes again starting to water. "Let's go now…"

In the back of his mind, Cory filled in the rest of her sentence. *In case I change my mind.*

While watching his mother's face, he became aware of the vague sensation of warmth on his left hand. He looked down to see Daphne's hands wrapped around it.

She looked up at him with big, wide eyes behind her dark glasses. "I'll come with you if you want."

His throat closed up. He didn't like subjecting her to the ugly parts of his life, but at the same time, he felt lost. More lost than the day as a kid when his favorite dog he'd been walking at the animal shelter had been adopted and taken to a new home before he'd had a chance to say goodbye. "Yeah. I'd like that."

"I don't think it's a good idea for me to leave my car here, since I don't know how long this will take. I'll follow you."

"Okay."

Without another word, he escorted his mother to his truck. He watched as Daphne got into her car and closed the door, then he headed for the rehab center.

After a few blocks his mother turned to him. "She seems like a nice young woman."

"Yeah, she is."

"It seemed quite brave of her to come here to talk to me. She had no idea what she would find."

It was true.

He didn't know why she'd come, but the bottom reason would be that it was because of him. "Yeah. It was pretty brave. She's been through some bad stuff."

"You must like her a lot."

He would marry her tomorrow if she said she would. "Yeah. I do."

"I hope I haven't ruined that for you. I've ruined so much of your life."

He squeezed the steering wheel as he spoke. "It hasn't been that bad. I've had a few rough spots, but they helped make me the man I am today, and I'm not a bad guy." He let the silence hang then turned to her when he stopped for a red light. "It was God's guidance that helped me with those rough spots, and God will help you now. All you have to do is ask."

"I'll think about it."

He nodded. The rehab center was a Christian organization, so he knew that she would be in good hands. Hopefully one day soon she would open her heart to God. When she started to ask questions, if he wasn't there to answer, it would be someone else when the time was right. Right now, she needed to take one small step at a time. For her to actually agree to rehab was a very big step.

They spent the rest of the way in silence, with only his favorite CD playing softly in the background. When they arrived, he escorted his mother out of the truck and led her to the office, where a woman was waiting for her.

The woman smiled and reached out to shake his hand. "It's best if you stay here, for confidentiality."

He didn't want to think that there were things his mother wouldn't want him to know, but there probably were. "I understand."

He looked at his mother. "I'll stay until you tell me to go."

"Thank you," the woman said. "That's best." Without another word, she led his mother into one of the offices and closed the door.

Cory sank into a chair. This was the moment he'd been waiting for, but now that it was happening, he felt lost.

The ring of the bell signified someone else had just entered the lobby. He turned to see Daphne walking in.

"What happens now? I've never done this sort of thing before."

Cory stood. "Me neither." He turned toward the office door where his mother was. No windows in the wall or the door ensured confidentiality of the person inside, which was probably a good thing. "The woman said to wait. I guess this is the moment where they outline what happens along with expectations and requirements, and my mother will either agree and sign up, or I take her home."

"I think she's going to do it." Daphne turned to him. "She was really sorry for everything. We had a really good talk."

Before he could respond, the door opened. His mother remained inside while the woman approached them. "She's going to stay. She asked if you can go to her place and bring her some clothes and make sure her car is locked. The five-day detox withdrawal session is going to be hard, so she wants to stay here so she doesn't change her mind. A lot of people do that." She dropped his mother's keychain in his hand. "You can leave a suitcase or bag at the front desk if I'm not here."

He stared at the keys in his hand. "I can do that." But his feet wouldn't move. He turned toward Daphne. "I'll go with you," she said before he needed to ask.

Chapter 13

For a while Daphne didn't say anything as Cory drove in silence. But as the silence continued, it nearly broke her heart to watch his face. He looked absolutely stricken.

"How would you like to stop over there for coffee?" She pointed out the window to a coffee shop. "I think we need to talk."

"Sure." He didn't say anything as he pulled into the lot and parked the truck.

She really didn't want coffee. She really wanted to talk to him when he wasn't driving. Before he could get out of the truck to run around to get the step for her, she reached out to wrap her fingers around his lower arm.

"Wait. We need to talk. I want to talk here, where it's private and you don't need to concentrate on driving. Your mom told me what really happened that night. I think you told me quite the edited version."

His face tightened. "She doesn't remember what really happened."

"Not all of it, but she remembered most. Why didn't you tell me that you were struck several times before you struck back, and that he threatened both you and your mother?" She gulped. "And that he had a knife?"

He pulled his arm out of her grip, wrapped both hands around the steering wheel and stared forward. "I've gone over it hundreds of times in my head, and each time it sounds like I'm making excuses, like it couldn't possibly have been like that. I've even doubted myself over the years. Maybe I'm remembering it the way I want to, to excuse my own guilt."

"You're not. Why can't you believe in yourself?"

He shrugged his shoulders. "I don't know to this day if I did the right thing. I seriously hurt him. I could have killed him. I even thought about it for a few seconds."

"But you didn't. And from what your mother said, it sounded like he was trying to kill you."

He turned to look at her.

"But he didn't. I won the fight, then instead of getting away from all that, my mother threw me out. She said I was ruining her life. I was trying to do something so her life wouldn't get ruined. I sure failed at that, too."

He turned back to stare blankly out the window.

"I'm so mixed up. She's finally in the right place, and I should be really happy, but I'm not. There are no guarantees that she'll straighten out."

"Want to pray about it?"

He gulped then once again looked at her. "Yeah. I do. That should have been the first thing I did, but everything has been moving so fast."

"We're not moving anywhere now." She extended one arm to emphasize that they were at a dead stop with the engine off, in the middle of a parking lot.

He sucked in a deep breath when she reached forward and held both his hands. "I'll start," she said, then lowered her head.

Daphne first prayed for his mother to open her heart and accept the help she would receive, and for strength to get through the hard parts. She then prayed for Cory; that he could release all his hurts and know that God had been with him then and was with him now.

When she went silent, Cory thanked God for his mother's change of heart and, to Daphne's surprise, he thanked God for her strength, support and friendship at a time when he needed it.

His heartfelt prayer nearly broke her heart, especially when he hesitated at the word "friendship."

This wasn't friendship. What they had was so much more.

If she doubted that she'd fallen in love with him, with all that she'd learned today, all those doubts had been erased. Now, hearing his words, she knew that without a doubt she'd fallen in love with Cory.

"Amen," she muttered, opening her eyes and releasing his hands.

He echoed her amen and his eyes fluttered open. He blinked multiple times and then wiped the back of his hand over his eyes.

She didn't know if it was possible to love anyone more than how she loved Cory.

Not waiting for him to recover, she pushed herself up to her knees, faced sideways on the seat and leaned toward him, then reached forward to cup his cheeks. "I'm going to kiss you, Cory Bellanger, because I love you."

His eyes widened, causing her to smile but not to stop what she was about to do.

Daphne moved toward him, closed her eyes and kissed the man she loved.

For a split second he stiffened, then his arms surrounded her and he kissed her back just the way she wanted.

The sound of footsteps beside the truck made her pull back from him. She didn't want another embarrassing incident of a stranger telling them to get a room.

But no one spoke. Instead, a young man turned and looked at them as he walked past, making an okay sign in the air with his fingers.

Her cheeks heated up as she looked at Cory, who didn't look the least bit embarrassed.

He reached forward and grasped both her hands in his larger ones. "Daphne Carruthers, you are the love of my life and keeper of my heart. Will you make me the happiest guy on earth and be my wife?"

* * *

Cory held his breath, hoping that in the confines of the cab of his truck, she couldn't hear his heart pounding. Since she'd said she loved him, he didn't think she should be taking so long to respond. Unless the answer was one he didn't want to hear.

Suddenly the reason for her not replying hit him like a sack of rocks.

They were inside a vehicle. The day her first boyfriend asked her to marry him, he'd taken her to his vehicle and attempted to rape her.

Cory dropped her hands and moved back, toward the driver's door. He didn't know whether he should tell her not to be afraid or to actually say the words that he wasn't going to attack her.

Her eyes widened as he hit the door with a thud, then welled up with tears. "You are so sweet. I'm not afraid of you. That's not what I was thinking." She jerked her head toward the front of the truck, to the boy who had walked past. Cory hadn't thought about him, nor had he actually looked at the young man.

Not only was he looking at them, he was standing with his phone poised, ready to take a picture of them, presumably when he kissed her again.

As soon as Daphne saw that he saw the guy with the phone, she motioned her head to the rear of the truck. Rather than turn his head, he looked in the mirror to see a second young man standing just behind his door with his arms spread akimbo in the air.

Daphne grinned. "I think they're waiting for a photo bomb. You know how teens are. Is this the way you want to remember the day you proposed, and the day I said I'd marry you?"

Cory grinned back. "If that's a yes, then yes. I do."

"Yes. That's a yes. Let's give them a photo they'll never forget."

Instead of embracing her, Cory leaned toward her. In the same way, she leaned toward him. When their lips met he raised one hand in the air and gave the photographer a thumbs-up.

As he did so, he couldn't help but smile, breaking their kiss. With their lips still touching, he kept smiling. "I'm going to ask him to send me a copy of that."

Daphne pushed herself back to a seated position. "And you know what? I want to send a copy to Rick. Right now."

Cory's smile dropped. Rick. "Do you think this will be a problem for him?"

Daphne shook her head. "I hope not. He'll come around. He just wants to protect me. But he'll find other ways to keep himself busy."

"Speaking of busy, we need to get that photo and get moving. We have a delivery to make and then we have plans to make."

Daphne smiled. "Yes, we do."

He gave her a quick peck on the cheek before dashing out of the truck to ask for a copy of that very special photo.

It only took a few minutes for the young man to send it to him, and he was back in the truck. Instead of starting the engine, he opened the photo on his phone and held it up for Daphne.

"I'm going to keep this with me and look at it whenever I get stuck doing desk duty."

"Not me."

His heart sank.

She took the phone from his hand and wrapped her other hand around his fingers. "Because I'm going to print it and frame it, and put it on my desk at work to keep forever." She leaned forward and kissed him again. "Right next to that picture of the bird with the red tummy."

"I like that."

"And one more thing. When we get our own house, I want to have his and hers bird feeders."

He couldn't help but smile; he thought his heart was going to burst.

As he looked one last time at the picture before he drove away, he noticed that she was wearing the same dress she'd worn to Brad and Kayla's wedding, where he'd been the best man. The day they'd arranged for their first date.

Now she wasn't just going to be dating the best man.

She was marrying him.

* * * * *

REQUEST YOUR FREE BOOKS!

2 FREE INSPIRATIONAL NOVELS
PLUS 2
FREE
MYSTERY GIFTS

Love Inspired

YES! Please send me 2 FREE Love Inspired® novels and my 2 FREE mystery gifts (gifts are worth about $10). After receiving them, if I don't wish to receive any more books, I can return the shipping statement marked "cancel." If I don't cancel, I will receive 6 brand-new novels every month and be billed just $4.74 per book in the U.S. or $5.24 per book in Canada. That's a savings of at least 21% off the cover price. It's quite a bargain! Shipping and handling is just 50¢ per book in the U.S. and 75¢ per book in Canada.* I understand that accepting the 2 free books and gifts places me under no obligation to buy anything. I can always return a shipment and cancel at any time. Even if I never buy another book, the two free books and gifts are mine to keep forever.

105/305 IDN F49N

Name	(PLEASE PRINT)	
Address		Apt. #
City	State/Prov.	Zip/Postal Code

Signature (if under 18, a parent or guardian must sign)

Mail to the Harlequin® Reader Service:
IN U.S.A.: P.O. Box 1867, Buffalo, NY 14240-1867
IN CANADA: P.O. Box 609, Fort Erie, Ontario L2A 5X3

**Are you a subscriber to Love Inspired books
and want to receive the larger-print edition?
Call 1-800-873-8635 or visit www.ReaderService.com.**

* Terms and prices subject to change without notice. Prices do not include applicable taxes. Sales tax applicable in N.Y. Canadian residents will be charged applicable taxes. Offer not valid in Quebec. This offer is limited to one order per household. Not valid for current subscribers to Love Inspired books. All orders subject to credit approval. Credit or debit balances in a customer's account(s) may be offset by any other outstanding balance owed by or to the customer. Please allow 4 to 6 weeks for delivery. Offer available while quantities last.

Your Privacy—The Harlequin® Reader Service is committed to protecting your privacy. Our Privacy Policy is available online at www.ReaderService.com or upon request from the Harlequin Reader Service.
We make a portion of our mailing list available to reputable third parties that offer products we believe may interest you. If you prefer that we not exchange your name with third parties, or if you wish to clarify or modify your communication preferences, please visit us at www.ReaderService.com/consumerchoice or write to us at Harlequin Reader Service Preference Service, P.O. Box 9062, Buffalo, NY 14269. Include your complete name and address.

LIDIR13R

REQUEST YOUR FREE BOOKS!

2 FREE INSPIRATIONAL NOVELS
PLUS 2
FREE
MYSTERY GIFTS

Love Inspired
HISTORICAL
INSPIRATIONAL HISTORICAL ROMANCE

YES! Please send me 2 FREE Love Inspired® Historical novels and my 2 FREE mystery gifts (gifts are worth about $10). After receiving them, if I don't wish to receive any more books, I can return the shipping statement marked "cancel." If I don't cancel, I will receive 4 brand-new novels every month and be billed just $4.74 per book in the U.S. or $5.24 per book in Canada. That's a savings of at least 21% off the cover price. It's quite a bargain! Shipping and handling is just 50¢ per book in the U.S. and 75¢ per book in Canada.* I understand that accepting the 2 free books and gifts places me under no obligation to buy anything. I can always return a shipment and cancel at any time. Even if I never buy another book, the two free books and gifts are mine to keep forever.

102/302 IDN F5CY

Name _____ (PLEASE PRINT)

Address _____ Apt. #

City _____ State/Prov. _____ Zip/Postal Code

Signature (if under 18, a parent or guardian must sign)

Mail to the **Harlequin® Reader Service:**
IN U.S.A.: P.O. Box 1867, Buffalo, NY 14240-1867
IN CANADA: P.O. Box 609, Fort Erie, Ontario L2A 5X3

Want to try two free books from another series?
Call 1-800-873-8635 or visit www.ReaderService.com.

* Terms and prices subject to change without notice. Prices do not include applicable taxes. Sales tax applicable in N.Y. Canadian residents will be charged applicable taxes. Offer not valid in Quebec. This offer is limited to one order per household. Not valid for current subscribers to Love Inspired Historical books. All orders subject to credit approval. Credit or debit balances in a customer's account(s) may be offset by any other outstanding balance owed by or to the customer. Please allow 4 to 6 weeks for delivery. Offer available while quantities last.

Your Privacy—The Harlequin® Reader Service is committed to protecting your privacy. Our Privacy Policy is available online at www.ReaderService.com or upon request from the Harlequin Reader Service.

We make a portion of our mailing list available to reputable third parties that offer products we believe may interest you. If you prefer that we not exchange your name with third parties, or if you wish to clarify or modify your communication preferences, please visit us at www.ReaderService.com/consumerschoice or write to us at Harlequin Reader Service Preference Service, P.O. Box 9062, Buffalo, NY 14269. Include your complete name and address.

LIHDIR13R